HOT SHOT

Also by Kevin Allman

Tight Shot

Kevin Allman

HOT SHOT

A Hollywood Mystery

St. Martin's Press ❧ New York

Library of Congress Cataloging-in-Publication Data

Allman, Kevin.
    Hot shot/Kevin Allman.
       p.   cm.
    ISBN 0-312-16866-7
    I. Title.
    PS3551.L462H68   1997
    813'.54—DC21   97-17825
                                           CIP

First Edition: April 1998

10 9 8 7 6 5 4 3 2 1

For Joanne Schmaltz—missing and missed

All my thanks to the following: Jack and Arline Allman, Hope Dellon, Daphne Hart, Helen Heller, Andrew Lerner, Yvonne Loiselle, Kelley Ragland, Jim Schmaltz, and Tom Yeend III.

What is more distasteful: the public's insatiable thirst for gossip and false intimacy, or the individual's longing for display, for absolution by publicity? It's a toss-up.

—Jonathan Yardley

Though today we inhabit an electrically charged and electronically connected planet, we remain creatures atavistically committed to the small scale. It's not surprising that we should adopt as our heroes only a few dozen men and women. Call them celebrities, call them gods and goddesses, they are the embodiment in our time of classical heroes.

—Steven M. L. Aronson

That's why they pay you the big bucks, Peaches.

—Jocelyn Albarian

ONE

1

WHEN THE PHONE RANG at 6:52 A.M., I should have let the machine pick up. The only person who might be calling that early would be either a creditor or my agent, Jocelyn. Still in a pre-caffeinated haze, I lunged for the receiver, stubbing my toe on the packing box marked BATHROOM STUFF.

"Good morning, Peaches."

Not a creditor—Jocelyn. On her car phone, too. Car phones are one of my pet peeves of the modern age, right up there with infomercials and Martha Stewart.

I sat down on BATHROOM STUFF to rub my sore toe. "Jocelyn, it might be ten to ten in New York, but out here it's not even seven in the morning."

"Didn't you know? I'm in L.A. I just got out of a breakfast meeting at Le Petit Couchon. Why is it that no one in Los Angeles can make a decent bagel? Never mind. Listen, Peaches. I just made us both a lot of money."

The last time Jocelyn said that, I ended up writing the "unauthorized biography" of a teen star whose life could have been summed up on a Trivial Pursuit card. Jocelyn's get-rich-quick projects were like those offers where you get an all-expense-paid vacation for touring some hellish time-share; it's always more of an ordeal than you'd planned, and the prize is never that good. But, like a fish who hits the rubber worm again and again, I can't resist the words "a lot of money." Hell, given the state of my bank account, I probably would have done it for a free bagel at Le Petit Couchon.

"What do I have to do?"

"You don't *have* to do anything, Kieran. But I just had breakfast with a publisher who thinks you'd be perfect for a project he's putting together." She allowed herself a dramatic pause. "I got you first crack at the Dick Mann story."

Dick Mann was the star of a wholesome situation comedy called *Mann of the Family*—a hokey half-hour with lovable blond twins and a sheepdog named Buttons in it. Last month Dick Mann had dropped dead from an overdose of a designer drug called Hot Shot. Now the rumor in the industry was that the sitcom dad was into prostitutes, kinky sex—and, for all I knew, carnal knowledge of Buttons.

"Another unauthorized biography?"

"Not an unauthorized biography, a *memoir*. By So-and-So, as Told to Kieran O'Connor. Completely equal billing. I insisted on that."

"Who's the so-and-so?"

"Felina Lopez. Remember her?"

"The hooker from the Vernon Ash case? She hasn't been around in five years."

"Well, she's back now, claiming that she had an affair with Dick Mann."

"Was he married back then?"

"Oh, he was married," Jocelyn said. "I think Betty Bradford

Mann might have even been pregnant. Juicy, juicy. Danziger Press is very hot on—"

"Danziger Press?" There was the catch. "Jeez. I don't know. I have to work in this town."

"Well, don't do me any favors, Kieran. I just thought you could use the money, you still being out of work and all."

" 'On hiatus' is the official term."

"Out of work is the reality, Peaches."

I'm a celebrity journalist. It's an occupation that didn't even exist a generation ago, but I expect it'll start showing up on high-school aptitude tests soon. For the last few years, I've written a party column for the big L.A. daily. It's a pretty good gig for a freelance writer, and the pay is decent, but I had been teetering on the abyss of burnout for about a year. Then came the incident at the premiere of a certain Memorial Day blockbuster, and I couldn't deny it any longer. I was in the throes of Post-Party Depression.

It was your standard premiere—screening and dinner, kiss-kiss and bullshit—but the head of the studio was on hand to cut a red ribbon with a pair of oversized prop shears. It was the kind of pompous occasion that always brought out my wiseass side, but I'm still not sure what got the movie kahuna so enraged: my observation that the scissors were taller than he was, or my description of him as "vertically challenged." At any rate, all hell broke loose, and I got called downtown for a meeting with my editor, Sally, and a studio publicist, whose head spun around like Linda Blair's in *The Exorcist* while he made you'll-never-work-in-this-town-again threats.

Sally stuck by me, but it got worse. The studio head pressured the suits upstairs and threatened to drop all their movie advertising. In the end, the paper kept the ads, I got banned for life from the studio's screenings, the pint-sized potentate got his pound of flesh, and I had a three-month suspension—unpaid.

Secure in the knowledge that nothing worse could happen, I went to bed that night only to be awakened by an earthquake. It was only a 4.9—no great shakes on the Richter scale—but it proved fatal to my dilapidated old apartment building on the Venice boardwalk. A crack appeared on the front wall the next morning, and by evening it had stretched from the courtyard to the roof. The next day the L.A. earthquake squad arrived and slapped some red CONDEMNED stickers all over the doors. Overnight homelessness.

For a while I had lived with my best friend, Jeff Brenner, and his new wife, but three was a crowd—particularly when one was an unemployed writer—so I had moved into Claudia's apartment.

Claudia and I had been dating for almost five years, though we'd actually been a couple for only about two of them. Some people are drawn together by sex, others by mutual interests. Claudia and I were attracted to each other's ambivalence. Both of us reacted to commitment like a vampire reacts to sunlight, so we approached cohabitation warily. Fortunately, Claudia was expanding the coffeehouse she owned in Venice and was rarely home these days, so I had plenty of time to wallow around the house, walk on the beach, and throw myself daily pity parties.

What got to me about my gig at the paper wasn't the fact that I was unhappy, but rather the knowledge that I had no *right* to be unhappy. I had a job that defined cushy, a weird but reasonably satisfying relationship with a weird but reasonably satisfied girlfriend, and my own byline twice a week: "Have Tux, Will Travel," by Kieran O'Connor.

After all, it wasn't my fault if people would rather read about a film premiere than about foreign policy. It wasn't my fault if Americans were more interested in the president of a record company than in the president of the United States. And it certainly wasn't my fault if the country was circling the drain while we were busy amusing ourselves to death.

Was it?

"Jack Danziger wants a meeting this afternoon. If you're not going to do it, let me know so I can find another gho—collaborator."

"Mmph." Under different circumstances, I might have said no, but having all your possessions in a stack of liquor cartons does tend to alter one's worldview. Being a belletrist to a bimbo like Felina Lopez wasn't exactly my dream, but neither was unemployment and homelessness.

I scratched my chest and looked at the packing boxes that were piled around Claudia's living room like a child's fort. "I don't know. It sounds good, Jocelyn, but—"

"Fine. Take this down. We've got a meeting this afternoon at two-thirty at Danziger Press. It's in the DuPlante Tower in Beverly Hills. Doheny and—"

"I know where it is, Jocelyn. I live here, remember? And I didn't say I was going to do it. Besides, I can't meet you today. I told Claudia I'd help her out at the new coffeehouse."

"Peaches." Jocelyn gave the word four world-weary syllables. "All right. You think about it. You let me know. I'm reachable at Le Bel Age. All right?"

"Okay."

"But meet me in the lobby of the DuPlante Tower at two-fifteen so we can go up together. All right?"

". . . All right."

"Oh, and Peaches, wear something nice."

What little I had that Jocelyn would consider "nice" was packed away somewhere in Box Mountain. I finally came up with an outfit that I thought would pass muster. The pants were nice enough, but the tie had a small stain at the bottom and my right sleeve was held together by a paper clip. It didn't look too bad—if you didn't look too closely.

On the way over to Danziger Press, I detoured down to Venice to see Claudia. I wanted to tell her the news about the book, and besides, I needed to borrow money for gas.

Claudia owned a coffeehouse that had become a little too successful in the last year; it was sending her into a tax bracket somewhere between personal trainers and action-film stars. Her accountant had recommended channeling the profits into a new venture. Thanks to the clean-and-sober movement, there were now more coffeehouses in Southern California than there were bars, so Claudia had decided to diversify, turning Café Canem into a combination coffeehouse, laundromat, and public Internet station.

The opening of the new Canem was only two weeks away, but it was hard to imagine the place being ready in time. A crew had knocked down the west wall, opening the space to the defunct Copies R Us next door, and a thin film of white dust coated everything. Power tools screeched. Workers were planing lumber, adding termitey clouds of sawdust to the chaos. I'd been helping out a little, sawing two-by-fours and painting the bathroom, but actual demolition was a little beyond my skill level.

Claudia was slumped in a banana-yellow hairdresser's chair in the middle of it all, a washtub of melting ice at her feet. She reached down and tossed me a cold Barq's. "I can't take my eyes off them for a second. I went up the street to get some sodas, and when I came back they were out in their truck watching *All My Children* on a portable TV."

"Well, it's coming along. Sort of."

She rubbed a handful of ice on her neck, looking at me suspiciously. "You're awfully dressed up for demolition work."

"I got a job, Claude. At least I think I've got a job." I told her about Jocelyn's call, emphasizing the "lot of money" part. "And you wouldn't believe who I'm doing the book with. Felina Lopez."

"Who's that?"

"You remember. The Vernon Ash case. Slut for the prosecution."

Claudia rolled her eyes. "Why would anyone want to read a book by someone like that? The Ash case was almost five years ago."

"She's claiming she had an affair with Dick Mann. And she's ready to spill the beans."

Claudia made a moue. "Sounds like a tabloid story, not a book."

"Hey, there's a big check involved. I can't afford to ask too many questions."

"How big?" Subtlety was never Claudia's M.O.

I hesitated. Jocelyn hadn't mentioned any hard figures, but I didn't want to tell Claudia that.

"Big enough for me to get out of your hair and into an apartment of my own."

"Must be big if you're wearing a suit," Claudia said.

"A paper clip on your cuff? Oh, Kieran," sighed Jocelyn.

"My good stuff's still in boxes. It was the only one I could find."

Jocelyn sighed again and looked around the lobby of the DuPlante Tower as if she expected to find a menswear shop tucked behind the elevators. I tugged on my jacket. The cuff was undetectable as long as I kept my arm pressed flat against my body. She wet one finger and tried to press down my cowlick.

I squirmed away. "Cut it out, Jocelyn. The hair is genetically uncontrollable. I'm black Irish."

Jocelyn, who was English, said, "Of that I'm only too well aware."

She produced a tortoiseshell compact and checked her teeth for lipstick. Jocelyn was wearing one of her usual negotiating outfits, an aggressive red Chanel suit with screw-you pumps and shoulderpads that could slice cheese. Nancy Reagan might have thought it a little severe.

When her teeth had been inspected and her stockings straightened, Jocelyn pushed a button. An elevator materialized as if it had been waiting just for her. On the way up, I said, "You never mentioned any figures."

"Didn't I?"

"No. You just said a lot of money." Driving over, I'd run some numbers in my head and came up with three different sums: what I wanted, what I'd take, and what I expected them to offer. "How much is a lot?"

"How much would you accept?"

I groaned. "Come on, Jocelyn. You work for me, not them, remember? Did Danziger mention any preliminary figures? A ballpark number?"

The doors glided open silently, revealing a reception area that could have been decorated by Jane Austen. A Helena Bonham Carter look-alike murmured into the telephone at a spindly-legged receptionist desk. On the far wall, behind an expanse of wine-colored carpet and antique furniture, silver letters spelled out DANZIGER PRESS.

Jocelyn leaned over and whispered a figure in my ear.

It was the amount I wanted and the amount I'd take—combined.

My eyebrows went up.

"I told you I'm good, Peaches."

2

THE RECEPTIONIST WORE A cloche and a pair of hip LA Eye-works glasses. Before she could snub us, Jocelyn snapped off our names, freeze-drying her 'tude with one sentence. It was like dipping baby's breath into liquid nitrogen.

"Just warming up," Jocelyn murmured as we sat down.

Looking at the lobby, drinking in the sight of so much old furniture bought with so much new money, I felt my moral compass taking a 180-degree turn. It wasn't just the sum Jocelyn had mentioned that got my cynical heart dripping like a Popsicle; it was the ease with which the deal had been made.

What a piece of work was Hollywood! Your agent has one breakfast with the right person, and you're set up for a year. So I wasn't Saul Bellow, but who was these days? And if I had to have a sleazy tell-all on my résumé, it might as well come from Danziger Press—the gold standard in the sleazy tell-all industry.

In L.A., selling out was just too easy. It was less *Doctor Faustus* than it was *Let's Make a Deal*.

Back in the conference room, waiting for Jack Danziger and Felina Lopez, Jocelyn wasted no time setting up. From her briefcase she extracted a heavy Mont Blanc pen and a portfolio covered in understatedly expensive hide, no doubt from some endangered species. She eyed the table and selected the seat that would give her the best psychological advantage. Jocelyn could give Lao-tzu pointers on the art of corporate war. I slumped in my chair, which was covered in silky gray leather. The conference room was just as plush as the lobby. Jack Danziger wasn't doing too bad for a man whose name was once a publishing-world punch line.

There were framed covers of various Danziger Press books on the walls, along with corresponding blowups of the *USA Today* best-seller list, featuring each title at No. 1.

Have You Reached a Verdict?: Inside the Deliberation Room at the Sunset Strangler Murder Case, by Juror 567

Keeping House: _____ and _____'s Maid Tells All About Hollywood's Most Famous Couple

Blow by Blow: The Private Diaries of a Tinseltown Call Girl

"Jocelyn," I said quietly.

"Hmm?" She had her portfolio open, making notes.

"What if I don't want my name on the book?"

Her pen stopped in midair. "What?"

"Couldn't I be a real ghost? Without my name attached? Just let Felina take the credit?"

"Kieran, are you mad? I spent half an hour this morning getting you that! And not some 'as told to' credit, Peaches! Full co-authorship!" She read from her notes. "The order and manner of credits given to said parties identified as the Proprietor of the Work shall read "Felina Lopez and Kieran O'Connor," with both names in the same-sized typeface in all editions of the Work—"

"I thought about it. I don't want it."

"Peaches . . ." For the first time since I'd known her, Jocelyn was nearly speechless. "Peaches, billing is *very* important. You live out here, you *know* that. Some people would kill for equal billing. It gives you more money, more leverage on your next book, more everything."

"I don't care. I don't—"

At that moment, Jack Danziger walked in, and Jocelyn stood up to greet him, shooting me a look that said: *We'll talk about this later.*

"Jocelyn, hello."

"Jack! This is Kieran."

"Love your column, really love it," Danziger told me. "Was just reading it the other day."

"Thanks." Obviously he hadn't even noticed its absence for the last few weeks. Judging from the lack of protest calls to my editor, neither had anyone else. He pumped my hand. Remembering my own office-supply cuff link, I dropped my hand under the table just as soon as Danziger had shook it with his Nautilus iron-man grip.

Danziger wore one of those flat-fronted Armani suits that look like silk armor, and had a portfolio tucked under his arm. He was a big man, but not fat; *strapping* was the word that came to mind. Lots of Hollywood dealmakers and desk jockeys pump absurd amounts of iron; it must have something to do with their clients' on-screen machismo.

"Felina's not going to be with us," Danziger said. "Her agent's on her way. Kitty just phoned."

Jocelyn's eyebrows went up like a window shade. Tardiness

was a cardinal sin in her book. Jocelyn was remarkably non-sexist when it came to revenge; she'd as soon have a woman's balls for breakfast as a man's.

"Kitty?" asked Jocelyn. "Kitty Keyes?"

"You two know each other?"

"No," said Jocelyn, dangerously demure. "But I've always wanted to."

So had I.

Until just a few years ago, Kitty Keyes had been a struggling talent agent. Not an agent, but a talent agent. An agent books movie stars and Broadway performers; a talent agent books birthday-party clowns and midget bowling teams and Ann Miller impersonators who tap-dance at car-wash openings. Kitty had all these, along with several former child stars whose puberty had killed their careers.

It was one of these postpubescents, Susie Quimby, who had revived Kitty's career. Arrested after trying to hold up a liquor store, Susie told the media that she'd been supporting herself by hooking out in San Bernardino. Awhile back, that might have put an end to any career she had left, but by the end of the week, Susie had more offers than she'd had in years.

Susie Quimby was the new wave, and Kitty Keyes knew it.

Soon after, Kitty dismissed her stable of has-beens and never-wases and founded Scandal, Inc., an agency that represented only the notorious. People laughed, but Kitty was turning a profit faster than Susie could turn a trick. Being bad was now big business.

"Kitty just phoned from the garage downstairs," soothed Danziger. "From her cellular."

"I'm here, I'm here," came a voice from down the hall. "I'm so sorry I'm late, but I just came from downtown; I swear I'll never get used to those one-way streets—"

Kitty Keyes burst in, looking rattled. Jack and I both stood up. Kitty stuck out her hand, and when I took it, she surprised me by pulling me to her and giving me a lipsticky kiss. She smelled like a box of old dusting powder.

With her strawberry-blond cloud of hair, prominent, horsey teeth, pink suit, and orange scarf, Kitty Keyes looked like an old Hollywood warhorse from the late-late show: Rhonda Fleming, maybe, or Dolores Gray. And when she opened her mouth, another actress came to mind: Billie Burke in *The Wizard of Oz*.

Kitty hadn't stopped rattling since she walked through the door. "This city has gotten so busy! Or maybe I'm just older than Adam's housecat—I can remember when you could drive from downtown to Beverly Hills in fifteen minutes . . ."

By the end of her monologue, Kitty had fussed herself into a chair directly across from Jocelyn, who had remained as quiet as a cobra in a basket until she interrupted gently: "Well, we don't have much time left. Shall we get down to it?"

The deal was straightforward boilerplate. Felina and I would be splitting the advance and any profits 60/40, with a graduated royalty schedule based on the number of books sold. There would be some background about Felina's Hollywood hooker days and some more about the Vernon Ash trial, but the bulk of the book would be about Felina's life as Dick Mann's mistress. Our contract called for a manuscript of approximately fifty thousand words, due one month after signing.

"A month?" I said. "To do research, interviews, *and* write fifty thousand words?" Claudia could forget about any help on the new coffeehouse.

"We're racing the clock. Dick Mann's already been dead a couple of weeks. And the tabloids are about to beat us to it. I've got a contact at *Celeb* who sent me a copy of next Monday's issue. Take a look at this."

Danziger opened his portfolio and passed us some color photocopies. The lurid cover was familiar to anyone who's ever been stuck in the ten-items-or-less line. Next to a picture of Dick Mann was a bright-red headline: TV DAD'S WILD SEX LIFE. The story was on page 3:

DICK MANN'S SECRET LIFE — DRUGS, DRINK, ORGIES

Hollywood Party Girl Tells All

by Gina Guglielmelli

"Dick Mann was into booze, drugs, and sex—the kinkier the better!"

In this exclusive *Celeb* interview, that's the shocking charge made by "Desiree," a Tinseltown hooker who claims she had an affair with America's favorite TV dad.

According to Desiree, she met the star of *Mann of the Family* when her exclusive prostitution service sent her to a Beverly Hills hotel to meet a client she knew only as Mr. M.

"When he opened the door, I recognized him right away," Desiree said. "He had requested a blonde in a white negligee. When I came in and dropped my coat, revealing the white negligee, his eyes lit up.

"We made love several times that night, stopping only to order room service. Dick was insatiable. I knew he was married, but it didn't seem to bother him.

"On my way out, he gave me a $400 tip in cash and said he'd see me again."

That was the first of several meetings, according to Desiree.

"On one occasion, he had me dress in a white nurse's uniform. He had a thing for white. Another time, he requested . . .

I quit reading. Sex fantasies, viewed from outside the bedroom, are always either screamingly funny or just mundane. Dick Mann's were in the latter category.

"Can you have a disk ready to go in four weeks?" Danziger asked me.

"I can try."

"Felina's already started jotting down a few things," Kitty murmured.

"Can you get down to Mexico in the next few days? Felina's eager to get started."

"Why are we doing it in Mexico?"

"Kieran's right," Jocelyn said. "Or can't your client come into the United States?"

"Of course she can. But she's insistent on doing it there. Which brings up another point," Kitty said. She cleared her throat. "Dear, I've got a question to ask you, and I'm not quite sure how to do it except to be blunt."

"Go ahead and ask," I said, puzzled.

"Well, then . . . what's your astrological sign?"

Jocelyn's eyebrows disappeared under her hairline. "Capricorn."

Kitty inhaled. "I was afraid of that."

"What, Capricorn is that bad?"

Danziger rolled his eyes. "Felina said she'd only do the book with a Libra or an Aquarius."

"She doesn't get on well with Capricorns or Tauruses," Kitty explained. She gave Danziger a worried glance.

Jocelyn tossed her Mont Blanc on the table. "Well, I'm a Feces with Asparagus rising," she said, "and I think this is preposterous. If Kieran's bloody birthday is enough to queer this deal—"

"Jocelyn—"

"—you've been wasting my time and my client's."

"Now, everybody just simmer down." Danziger tried for a smile and didn't quite make it. "I'm sure we can work this out. Kitty, what if Kieran tells Felina he's a, whatchamajigger—"

"A Libra or an Aquarius?" Kitty blinked. "I don't know. Dear, do you think you could pull off impersonating a Libra or an Aquarius?"

"Hey, I'll be a Libra for a month," I said, and Jocelyn snorted.

More warning bells. At that point, a smarter person would have called the whole thing off. I had no idea that by the end of the month one person would be dead and I'd be in hiding. All I was thinking was, For that kind of money I could be a lesbian Scientologist.

3

DANZIGER'S OFFICE HAD MADE reservations for me at someplace called the Hotel del Toros in downtown Tijuana. According to Kitty Keyes, I was to meet Felina at five on the dot in the hotel restaurant. It seemed awfully cloak-and-dagger to me.

"Drama queen. She thinks she's Deep Throat," was Claudia's assessment. We were standing in front of Café Canem, saying our good-byes.

"Interesting choice of words." I pecked her on the cheek. Neither one of us was very kissy, especially in public. "I feel guilty leaving you with this place half-finished."

Claudia kicked me in the shin. "You've got a job to do. Besides, face it, Kieran. You're not exactly Mr. Home Improvement."

"See you next week."

In the back of my newly rented car I'd packed several changes of clothes, my laptop, two tape recorders, forty blank cassettes, several notebooks, my research materials, a Spanish-English dictionary, and six gallons of bottled water. The water was a precautionary measure. I didn't want to spend my Danziger-paid days holed up in a hotel with the squirts.

When I was younger, Tijuana was scurvy, the civic equivalent of a dive bar. Underage kids went there to drink cheap beer and get the clap, while older folks bought ugly trinkets and got their photos taken on the back of scrofulous burros. In the last few years, though, Tijuana had changed its image. Southern California magazines were always praising it as a hip day trip, a place with good music clubs, inexpensive food, and shopping bargains. The shopping I could do without, but I did like ceviche and margaritas.

Billboards lined both sides of the freeway, and industrial chimneys rose to my right in a ziggurat maze of refineries and factories. Some of the factories had flames leaping out of their chimneys, hazy under the yellow-white ball of hell in the sky. Palm trees stuck their heads out of the smog, matches waiting to ignite. In the distance, a billboard from some now-failed S&L delivered the news: ninety-eight degrees at 9:47 A.M. This was the real Southern California, the one they never put on the postcards.

After the hills of Irvine rolled by, the 405 merged with I-5, and the views got prettier. Even the chain outlets were white stucco, with terra-cotta roofs and splashes of scarlet bougainvillea. Another few miles, and I was driving along the Pacific Ocean. The sky looked cleaner, and I was thinking that Southern California wasn't such a bad place to live after all.

Then I saw the yield sign on the side of the freeway: a yellow diamond with the silhouettes of running human beings.

Warning. Human crossing.

I was getting close to Mexico.

Since the lines at the return inspection station could be long, and American car insurance isn't valid in Mexico, I decided to park in San Ysidro and walk across the border.

Tijuana might have changed, but San Ysidro hadn't. It was still a weatherbeaten collection of dingy motels, fast-food outlets, and U-Park lots that advertised daily and weekly rates. I pulled into the first U-Park I saw, grabbed my bags, and said a silent prayer to whatever gods are in charge of broken windows and stolen hubcaps.

The border was just down the street, looking like a toll plaza. Even though it was only noon on a Friday, cars were lined up for a mile at the return inspection station. Border guards threaded through the traffic, letting their drug dogs sniff at tires. Heat waves rose from the road, baked by a urine-yellow sun. The pedestrian entrance was next to the motor crossing—nothing more than a dirty orange turnstile, like something you'd find at a dilapidated amusement park.

Welcome to Mexicoworld, I thought, and went through the turnstile.

The Hotel de Toros wasn't exactly the Four Seasons. My room was Spartan and threadbare as a dorm, decorated with faded prints of matadors and picadors sticking it to the bulls. It smelled of mildew and air freshener. A crack in the shower door was mended with duct tape. At least the phone worked, the linens were clean, and there was a bottled-water dispenser in the hall—a concession to gringo stomachs. I sacked out for a couple of hours before I went down to meet my co-writer.

I was there at five. Felina wasn't. Nor was she there at five-fifteen or five-thirty. At quarter to six, I went out to the lobby to use the phone. The receptionist at Danziger Press said that Jack Danziger had left for the day, and all I got at Kitty Keyes's office was a chirpy voice requesting that I leave a message.

"Señor O'Connor?"

It was the kid from the front desk. He held out an old-fashioned manila envelope, the kind with a string instead of a clasp. It bulged in the middle like a football.

"A lady came by and left this for you. I rang your room, but you weren't in."

I took the envelope. "What did the lady look like?"

"*Muy bonita.* Long hair. And these." He grinned and held his hands at chest level, curling his fingers.

Either my visitor had breast implants or severe arthritis.

Back in my room, I cracked a bottle of water, found a *tejano* station on the clock radio, and sat down with Felina's manuscript. On the back cover I discovered a hastily scribbled note:

> *I had an appointment and couldn't wait. So here's the book.*
> *Read it and let me now what you think, alright?*
> *I'll meet you back here at 11 tomorrow.*
> *Felina Lopez*

I frowned as I undid the string. This did not look promising.

Inside was a mishmash of notebook paper and yellow sheets from a cheap legal pad, written in longhand with at least three different ink colors, lots of marginalia, cross-outs, and clumpy blobs of Liquid Paper that kept sticking the pages together. Grains of sand fell out of the spine of the folder. It didn't take the Hardy Boys to figure out that she'd probably written it during long afternoons at the beach.

I sprawled across the bed, turning the pages slowly, trying to decipher her sloppy handwriting, her sloppier transitions, and her impenetrable spelling. When it got dark, I turned on the lamp and kept going. Outside, noise began to float up from Avenida Revolución: hard-driving rock, car horns, hoots and hollers from the *turistas*.

When I finally turned the last page, I checked my watch. Nine-thirty. After midnight Manhattan time. Too bad. This was an emergency.

I dialed Jocelyn's home-slash-office in Chelsea. The machine picked up.

"Houston," I said, "we have a problem."

"It can't be that bad."

"It is."

It was four in the morning, Tijuana time, but I hadn't been able to do more than doze and channel-surf.

"Well, what's the problem?" I heard a coffee grinder running at the other end of the phone. "Isn't there enough on Dick Mann?"

"There's plenty. But it's all good. She loves him, Jocelyn."

"She loves—"

"Pardon me. Not loves. She *worships* him. It's the romance of the ages. It's *The Bridges of Madison County* with a hooker in it."

"Oh, dear . . ."

"You bet 'Oh, dear.' It's the sensitive tale of an innocent young sex worker—her phrase, not mine—who's been mistreated by every man in Hollywood until the wonderful Dick Mann taught her what real love meant."

There was a long silence. Jocelyn finally said, "This complicates things."

"Complicates? It ruins things! Jack Danziger is expecting fifty thousand words of dirt on Dick Mann. What the hell are we going to do, Jocelyn?"

"I'm not going to do anything. *You're* going to have to get her to talk, Peaches."

"Even the best writer in the world couldn't turn a love story into *Dickie Dearest*, Jocelyn. And I'm not the—"

"Shit."

"What?"

"I got coffee grounds all over my new Donna Kieran, Karan. I mean Kieran." Jocelyn wasn't at her best in the mornings. "And I've got a breakfast meeting in midtown in forty-five minutes."

"What am I supposed to do?"

"Just fix it the best you can. That's what they're paying you the big bucks for, remember? Work with her. You can be diplomatic when you have to. You're meeting with her today, yes?"

"Yeah. But I've got a bad feeling about this."

"All right. All right. Meet with her. Give it a day or two. If you're still getting nowhere, I'll put in a call to Jack and have him talk to Kitty Keyes. And if that doesn't work, I'll call Kitty and have a word with her myself. That's the best I can do. Do you feel better now?"

"Yeah," I said. I didn't.

"Good. Now let me go put on my face. Call me after you meet with Felina. And don't panic, Peaches. It's all fixable."

I hung up the phone and switched on the TV moodily. A

cheesy cubic-zirconium necklace was rotating on a plinth. How did we ever get along without herringbone necklaces and porcelain unicorns?

Normally the Home Shopping Channel knocks me out faster than Sominex, but thin blue streaks of daylight were coming through the windows before I finally drifted off to sleep.

Eleven came and went. I bought a copy of the San Diego paper from the desk clerk and staked out a chair in the lobby. At eleven-twenty, I decided to give her ten more minutes before I called Jocelyn again. At 11:29, she walked through the door.

Felina Lopez was thinner than I remembered, but she was still a head-turner. She wore a man's denim shirt, unbuttoned to show a good bit of implant décolletage. A pair of stovepipe jeans was tucked into leather boots. Over her shoulder was a large leather satchel.

She scanned the lobby briefly before spotting the tape recorder on the table. I'd left it there on purpose—a beacon, a signal, a reporter's equivalent of the red carnation in the buttonhole.

"Hi. I'm Kieran O'Connor," I said, standing up.

"Hello." Not enthusiastic. From the look she was giving the lobby, she had expected something a little more luxe.

"We met briefly a couple of times before. Once at the premiere of *Bad Medicine*, and again at that party for Steve Martin at the museum. You were with—"

"I remember."

"You do?"

"Not you. The party."

Felina stared at me. It was a look I'd seen on too many Hollywood types, a look that analyzed you from one point of view only: *What can this person do for me?* And from the purse of disapproval at the edges of her Lancômed lips, the answer was: *Not much.*

She looked around the lobby again and shook her head. "I can't work here."

"Where do you want to go?"

"I don't know. I don't live in Tijuana." She shrugged. "We'll find somewhere."

Out on Avenida Revolución, tourists blocked the sidewalk. The exhaust fumes were stifling. Felina moved off down the sidewalk without a word. I had trouble keeping up with her long legs, and she didn't wait for me.

Avenida Revolución was pretty tatty by day. Past the jai alai arena, there were a few tired-looking titty bars, but most of the joints on Revolución were Americanized Mexican. Pastel-colored, with wooden parrots in the windows, they all had names like Jose O'Brien's and Paco MacTavish's. In this district, at least, Tijuana's renaissance seemed limited to capturing the college-kid dollar.

Felina detoured off the main drag after a block, cutting through an open-air *mercado* where a raggedy-ass band of mariachis was playing *ranchero* songs for a group of tourists. Heat waves and a nauseating smell rose from a nearby pushcart where a man peddled frankfurters and *chicharónes*. We wove our way through a maze of little stands and vendors hawking leather purses, plaster cobras, rosaries, Kahlua and tequila, genuine faux snakeskin belts, and Elvis walking hand in hand with Jesus on black velvet. Claudia would have loved it.

I spotted a restaurant across the street. "How about there?"

Felina shook her head and kept going.

The street narrowed, and I began to notice dilapidated storefronts hung with signs that advertised FARMACIA. People with everything from cancer to AIDS made drug runs to TJ for dubious *prescripcións* that were unavailable in the United States. Laetrile was still popular, but now the *farmacias* also did a big business in kombucha mushrooms, black-market AZT, protease inhibitors, and Rohypnol.

Another block, and suddenly the asphalt turned to dirt and the signs were all in Spanish. The street was busy, but I didn't see another American. Passersby were beginning to stare, and I wasn't sure what attracted attention: Felina's figure or the gringo trotting along beside her.

In the middle of the next block, she stopped so quickly I almost ran into her back.

We were standing in front of a low-slung building: lemon-yellow with red enamel trim. Red wooden silhouettes of roosters hung next to old-fashioned saloon doors. I could hear *tejano* music and male voices inside. A hand-painted sign over the entrance read EL GALLO ROJO. The Red Rooster.

"Here," Felina said.

"You been here before?" I asked dubiously. For all we knew, this was a cockfighting palace or the meeting hall for a Tijuana tong.

Felina shook her head no. She looked hypnotized. "The rooster is my power animal."

"What?"

"I was born in the Year of the Rooster." She reached out to stroke one of the silhouettes on the building's face. "It's always an important year."

"Uh-huh," I said. Whatever. The woman was giving me the creeps.

Felina walked through the saloon doors without a word. I followed her, hanging back a couple of paces.

No cockfighting, I noted with relief. The Gallo Rojo was just a working-class restaurant and bar, with oilcloth-covered tables and battered wooden booths. It smelled of lard and cumin. A long bar against one wall was trimmed in tinsel and Christmas lights, with a large plaster madonna standing guard over the tequila bottles. Behind the pass-through window that led to the kitchen, an old woman was patting dough into ovals and turning them onto a griddle. We took the only available booth, right near the two doors that read DAMAS and CABALLEROS.

Time to butter the lady up. "So tell me about roosters."

"It's a sign of change. Every twelve years, *el gallo* brings change and cataclysm. The Nazi Party came into existence during the Year of the Rooster. Twelve years later, World War Two ended. Twelve years later, Sputnik was launched and the Space Age began. Twelve years later, people walked on the moon. Twelve years after that, AIDS was discovered."

"How interesting." What a pile of cock-a-doodle-do.

Up close, Felina looked forty, maybe even forty-five. Her tawny mane was still thick and shiny, but spiderwebs were inlaid around her eyes, her hands were marked with blue veins, and her neck was turning to crepe. Her olive skin was stretched tightly across her cheek implants, which stood out in bas-relief like knife slashes.

"Those homemade tortillas smell great. Are you going to have some?"

"Lard," Felina said ominously. "Lard."

So far we had all the rapport of two eighth-graders thrown together by a teacher and told to complete a science project.

The waiter came over. He and Felina started talking in rapid-fire Spanish. My language skills are at the "*¿dónde está la biblioteca?*" level. I couldn't follow a word. When the waiter looked at me, I shrugged and said, "*Dos.*"

Felina reached into her purse and brought out a black velvet drawstring bag. From it she removed several small carved stones that looked like onyx, quartz, alabaster. She arranged the stones on the table in a semicircle in front of her. She rearranged, fussed, rearranged again. When she was done, it looked like a tiny Stonehenge.

"Your stones are pretty," I said.

"Not stones. They're Zuni fetishes."

"Like good-luck charms?"

"Sort of."

"Can I look at them?"

She shrugged. I picked up a white alabaster blob. Up close, a bird revealed itself: sharp beak, carved feathers smooth against its back. I ran my finger over its coolness.

"The eagle," she said. "*La águila.* A symbol of strength, fierceness, protection."

"He protects you?"

"I protect myself. The eagle is a symbol. My familiar."

"I see," I said, trying to keep my voice neutral. Power animals. Familiars. Hollywood New Age types got on my nerves. I wasn't sure whether it was the crass selfishness couched in spirituality or the Chinese-menu aspect of New Age that bothered me. It wasn't that I didn't have an open mind; it just didn't catch every trendy stray breeze.

"I didn't want another writer on my book," she said.

"Oh."

"I spent six months working on my story. My agent was the one who said I needed a co-writer."

"Why didn't you take it to another publisher?"

"Because I listened to *la águila*," she said, touching the eagle. "He told me that I wouldn't get my story out until I teamed up with someone else. And he told me about you."

I was over the New Age mysticism. "And what did he tell you, Felina?"

"You don't want to be here. You don't want to be writing this book with me." Her eyes never left mine. "You think it's sleazy. Cheap. So why are you doing it?"

"Same reason you are," I told her. "Money."

"Are you a good writer?"

"You tell me when we're done."

"How did Jack pick you?"

"My agent set it up." Thrust, parry. Thrust, parry.

"You could have turned it down."

"I'm just a boy who can't say nnn—nnn—nnn—"

She didn't laugh. Neither did *la águila*.

The waiter brought over two wooden bowls filled with romaine. He poured olive oil into a glass dish, broke an egg, separated the yolk in one economical motion, and added it to the oil. In quick succession, he cut a lemon, squeezed the juice, and added Worcestershire and fresh crushed garlic. Last was a whole fresh anchovy, which he diced with the casual malice of a sushi

chef. A few quick motions with a whisk, and the mixture became a glossy dressing, which he poured over one salad. Then
he added fresh ground pepper and put the bowl in front of me.
He set the plain bowl of romaine in front of Felina and left.

"No dressing?" I said.

"I bring my own." Felina reached into her bag again. She
pulled out a three-finger leather cigar case, a couple of vitamin
bottles, and several glassine envelopes full of herbs before she
found the Ziploc she was looking for. It was filled with what
looked like a thick, lumpy vinaigrette. She poured the goo over
her lettuce. It smelled like a piece of Gorgonzola that had been
left out of the refrigerator for a day.

"Well," I said. "Shall we get to it?"

"We're going to have to add some things, do a little restructur-
ing, but overall it's all there."

"You didn't like that section?"

"No, it worked fine. But it'll work better—turn back a couple—there. See?"

She bent her head over, and I could smell the garlic on her
breath. "Oh. Yeah."

It was an hour later, and I was beginning to think maybe the
book was salvageable—even if it might not be as rosy as Felina
painted it or as dirty as Danziger wanted it to be. To my surprise,
Felina accepted the few soft criticisms I lobbed at her, and suggested improvements on her own. We were getting along just
fine.

And then I brought up Dick Mann's drug use. "I know you
don't want to talk about that," I said gently. "But it's part of the
story."

"Why do we have to bring that up?"

"It's already been brought up for us. Look at this." I handed her the *Celeb* article.

She looked at it for a long moment. "Oh, God," she said. "Sloan Baker."

"Who?"

"Sloan Baker. We worked at the same agency. I knew she was double-dealing customers to the tabs." She tapped *la águila* on the table nervously. "This is just like something Sloan would do. She probably got a few thousand for it."

"Did Sloan sleep with Dick Mann, too?" I took her silence as a yes. "How do you know?"

"I was there. But that was at the beginning. After that it was just Dick and me. And I don't want to write about that, anyway," she said sharply.

"I know. I know. But if you don't, no one will read the rest of your story. Dick Mann's personal life is going to become public knowledge very soon. If you're not honest, people like this"—tapping the tabloid—"will get the last word."

Felina was quiet for a moment. "I'm not just thinking about Dick and me. There's a child involved," she said.

"His son?"

"Betty Mann never did anything to me. I'm just not the same . . ."

"Give it some thought. We can tell the whole truth without making it exploitative," I said earnestly. "It is called *Mann's Woman*, after all. If you're going to tell the good times, you have to tell the bad times, too. Right?" I was full of more shit than a bag of Bandini.

Felina opened her cigar case, thinking. She took out a

panatela and used a pair of curved silver scissors to behead the cigar. It was a strangely elegant gesture, feminine and masculine at the same time.

"You don't eat lard, but you smoke?"

"These, you don't inhale. My father taught me how to smoke. He was a cigar roller." She produced a long wooden match and touched it to the head of the cigar, the flame just kissing the tip. A rich fragrance drifted up, a plume of spice and leather.

"It smells good."

"Romeo y Julieta. From Cuba." She pronounced it Koo-ba, not Kyew-ba. "I taught Dick how to smoke cigars, too."

"I read that. I liked that detail."

"I just don't want it to look like . . . Cristo . . ."

"Look like what?"

"I was a different person back then. I had bought into the L.A. scene. Drugs, parties. Lifestyles of the rich and famous. But living with Vernon Ash changed me. After a while, I knew that I had two choices: leave or die. Dick was the one who con-vinced me to leave him."

"That wasn't in the book," I noted.

She nodded. "Dick was a client of mine for sex and a client of Vernon for drugs."

"Was that unusual?"

"No. We had a few people like that. I got 'em coming and Vernon got 'em going." She laughed nervously, puffing smoke. "That was Vernon's joke. Can't you see why I don't want to—"

"Wait a minute. You were working while you were Ash's girlfriend? He wasn't jealous?"

"Are you kidding? The agency I worked for catered to movie stars, athletes, Saudi money. Most of them used drugs. I was their connection to Vernon, and I was Vernon's connection to them."

"Did Dick Mann use a lot of drugs?"

"No! A little coke here and there. Once in a while some 'ludes. He told me he'd tried Hot Shot before, but he didn't like it."

"And Vernon got them for him?"

"Oh, yes."

I rubbed my eyes, trying to keep my voice steady. "Felina," I said, "why didn't you put any of this down in the book?"

Felina opened her mouth, as if to say something defiant, but nothing came out. I waited. She shrugged. I tried another tack.

"Great. You've got the love story down. Now we just have to add some of the—the background. Okay?"

Like a little girl: " 'Kay."

"I made a list of questions. Feel up to answering a few?"

She stared into a corner of the restaurant, where a plaster Madonna stood in an old bathtub, arms outstretched.

"Felina?"

"I guess," she said.

When I got back to the Hotel del Toros, I had two and a half hours of tape in my recorder. I also had a message from Jocelyn. She could barely control the smugness in her voice when I told her about the afternoon.

"Don't crow," I told her.

"So what did she tell you?"

"Some interesting stuff about Vernon Ash. They shared clients. Quite a team. He supplied the drugs and she supplied the—you know."

"What about Betty Bradford Mann? We need some juicy bits on her, Peaches, but nothing litigable."

"Not a lot yet. Felina never met her. She said that back then Dick was in a career lull. He hadn't had a good part in five years. *Mann of the Family* didn't come along for another year or two. Betty was the TV star. Felina says they were separated then—"

"Dick and Betty Mann were separated? I didn't know that."

"Not physically. They were still living in the same house, but they weren't sleeping together. Or so she claims."

Jocelyn snorted. "There's no one dumber than a woman in love with a married man. How many washed-up actors would leave their rich and successful wives for some hooker? Even with California's community property laws, a good divorce lawyer would submarine him." Jocelyn had personal experience with divorce law; when her husband left her and moved to Seattle, she did a little submarine job of her own. "So. When are you meeting next?"

"Tomorrow morning at nine."

"See how everything worked out? I knew it couldn't be as bad as you thought, Peaches. Felina needs the money from this book as badly as you do. And Danziger is drooling all over that horrible Armani suit of his. Did I tell you there was an item about the project in this morning's *Biz*? I'm sure he leaked it himself."

"Was my name mentioned?" More than ever, I didn't want my name on the project—except on the pay-to line of the royalty check. Still, I had to admit to a frisson at the thought of my name linked to a big deal in the trade-industry daily.

"No, you're still anonymous, Peaches. But don't you see? It ups the stakes for all of us. This is going to come off. Trust me."

When I hung up, I had a slimy feeling I couldn't shake. It was only five o'clock. I didn't feel like sitting around the hotel or strolling the streets of Tijuana, so I walked back over the border and drove into San Diego. I stopped at the first multiplex off the freeway and bought a ticket for the next feature without even noticing what the movie was.

No matter how you sliced, diced, or julienned it, I was as big a sleaze as Felina, if not more so. The worst part was that I still wasn't sure I could give Jack Danziger what he wanted.

Felina may have been a whore, but at least her clients got what they paid for.

That's why they pay you the big bucks, Peaches.

I popped a Jujyfruit disconsolately. Pinocchio had Jiminy Cricket. I got Jocelyn Cricket. My anti-conscience.

Nine o'clock. I bought a copy of the San Diego paper from the desk clerk and read it while slumped in a squishy chair in the lobby. At nine-thirty, Felina still hadn't shown. At ten, I left a note with the clerk and went to get breakfast at the Denny's down the street. The *huevos rancheros* tasted just like the ones at the American Denny's—which is, I guess, the whole point of Denny's. I lingered over coffee until 10:45 before strolling back to the hotel. Felina could be the one to wait for a change.

Only she still wasn't there.

A vague foreboding—a pre-premonition—prickled under my collar.

There was an old-fashioned phone booth in the corner of the lobby. I called Jocelyn, got her machine, and left a terse message. At Kitty's office, I got a maternal-sounding secretary who clicked her tongue and promised to give Ms. Keyes my message "just as soon as she sashays in the door."

I hung up, feeling my breakfast congeal in my stomach. Almost two hours late.

She wasn't coming.

If I left for L.A. now, I could be home by mid-afternoon. Jack Danziger could keep his money, Felina could have her manuscript back, and Kitty could find a ghostwriter who was more astrologically compatible than I was.

Back in my room, I was throwing shirts and notebooks into my suitcase when I came across the folder with Felina's manuscript. Remembering something, I took off the rubber bands and opened it to the title page.

There it was, in the bottom right-hand corner. *Felina Lopez, 2 Puesta del Sol, Via del Paraiso, B.C.* No phone number, though. Felina probably couldn't afford one.

I checked my watch. Eleven-fifteen. Even if Via del Paraiso was an hour down the coast, I could drive down, beard the lady in her beach shack, give her back the manuscript and a few well-chosen words, and be back in Santa Monica in time to surprise Claudia for dinner.

The desk clerk at the hotel gave me a map of upper Baja. It was in Spanish, but I found Via del Paraiso—a tiny dot on the coast just north of Ensenada, a straight shot down Highway 1.

Back in San Ysidro, I bailed my car out of the U-Park. It was intact, except for a big smear of seagull shit on the windshield. I stopped at a Shell station right before the border and filled up. I didn't trust the Mexican gasoline any more than I did the water. After crossing the border and paying my toll, I headed down the coast.

Just out of TJ was the resort town of Rosarito Beach. The last time Claudia and I had been down, it was a sleepy place with cheap grub and cheaper accommodations, but the Jose O'Brien's and Paco MacTavish's of the world had invaded. Why did people travel just to go someplace they could have gone at home?

A few miles farther, and the Pacific spread out to the right, a more brilliant blue than the dirty water of Santa Monica Bay. Seafood stands appeared on outcroppings over the rocks. Tourists sat on picnic benches right by the highway, eating huge plates of lobster and boiled corn. A parasailor appeared on the horizon, being dragged through the sky by a skiff. Sunlight glittered like dimes on the water. I passed a hamlet called La Misión and kept going.

The sign was so small and weatherbeaten that I almost missed it: VIA DEL PARAISO and an arrow. I turned off the highway and found myself on what wasn't even a street, just a paved road heading toward the water. No Jose O'Brien's or Paco MacTavish's here.

No street signs, either. I bumped along the road, passing a scattering of stuccoed shacks, each of which had a truck up on blocks in the front yard. One building had a hand-painted shingle tipped crazily toward the road: PELUQUERIA. Barbershop. I wondered who trimmed Felina's leonine mane. Did Via del Paraiso have its own José Eber?

Right before the beach, the blacktop dribbled out into a dusty intersection. To the right was an unpaved little street that threaded through a collection of seaside shacks. Smoke from a chimney or a cooking fire smudged the sky. To the left, another paved road climbed a small rise. The houses along the bluff were nicer. I could even see the top of a satellite dish behind one of the homes, a bristly steel sea urchin.

Uptown and shantytown, neatly cleaved by the main road: economic apartheid in action.

Which way to go? I couldn't imagine Felina being able to afford the houses on the hill. But could she really be living in the shantytown? Poverty was one thing for a Hollywood hooker. Third World living was another.

I got out of the car. The salt air hit me like a splash of aftershave. But something felt odd, and I couldn't quite place it.

Down by the fork in the road was a seabeaten street sign half-covered by a stand of palms. I got the manuscript, locked the car, and walked over to check out the sign. Rust had eaten at it mercilessly, but beneath the orange freckles I could make out that the shantytown road was Salida del Sol; the bluff road, Puesta del Sol. Sunrise and sunset.

So Felina was living on the hill after all. Maybe the houses on the bluff belonged to American expatriates and retirees, lured by the beach and the weak Mexican economy. Hell, if Felina could afford to live here, it couldn't be that expensive. I wondered how the locals viewed the invasion of the gringos.

Then it hit me, the source of my odd feeling: I hadn't seen

a single person in Via del Paraiso. More than that, I hadn't heard a sound.

I stood and listened, but all I heard was the rush of the sea wind. This place was the Twilight Zone.

Shaking off my jitters, I began walking up Puesta del Sol. The first house was number 24 and the second 22. Felina had to live at the end of the road. What I had assumed were the fronts of the houses were actually the backs; the fronts faced the Pacific. I passed kitchen doors, garage doors, and garbage cans. Still no one anywhere.

After 14, the road made another sharp rise that left me panting. I came upon a weatherbeaten wooden staircase, which zigzagged down the bluff toward the beach through a thicket of purple ice plant. The sand was as deserted as the streets.

A couple hundred more feet, and I was relieved to hear a few voices around the next switchback. I made the turn and stopped dead.

Puesta del Sol ended in a little cul-de-sac of three homes. Twenty or thirty people were standing in the road in front of the biggest house, a spread that wouldn't have been out of place in Laguna or Malibu. I took in the landscaping, the red tile roof, the satellite dish. Back in Santa Monica, this would be nearly a million dollars. The house stretched down the bluff in a series of wooden terraces angled to catch the sun and the view.

There were a number of Americans in the crowd. Though they were dressed casually, they all had the Southern California good-life look: brown skin, white teeth, flat tummies. To the side was a group of Mexicans—the residents from down the hill, no doubt. Most of them looked worried. One old woman threaded a rosary between her fingers.

What the hell were they staring at? I skirted the crowd and moved around to the side.

Three Ensenada police cars had made a barricade in front of the garage door. A mustachioed cop talked into a radio. Behind him, two men in coveralls were coming out of 2 Puesta del Sol, carrying something.

A stretcher. With a green plastic bag on top of it.

Next to me, the old woman fingered her rosary. Her lips moved, but no sound emerged.

"FORCE MAJEURE? THAT'S PREPOSTEROUS, Jack. Despite what happened to Felina—and it's a tragedy, I'm well aware of that, we're all well aware of that, that's completely beside the point, completely—we have a book here."

Jocelyn's agitated voice was coming out of a square black box on the table in the Danziger Press conference room. I half expected it to start hopping around the room like a cartoon.

"We have a manuscript. We have hours and hours of interview tape. We have Kieran ready and raring to go. *Force majeure*, acts of God, none of this is relevant."

"Death is an act of God, Jocelyn." Danziger sounded tired.

"Of course it is," said the Jocelyn box. "But Felina fulfilled her obligation. She got her story down. The rest was up to Kieran. Let him do his job."

Even by Jocelyn's rip-'em-to-shreds standards, this was really pushing it. Felina hadn't been dead twenty-four hours, and she was bucking to keep the project in play.

I sagged in my chair. The ride home had been physically and emotionally exhausting. By the time I hit Orange County, the traffic was metallic sludge and my A/C had conked out. I spent the last fifty miles with my window down, and now had a sunburn on my left arm that looked like radiation poisoning. There hadn't been time to go home and change before I had to meet Danziger for our powwow. My butt ached, my lungs burned, and the back of my shirt was still wet from the long drive.

Danziger didn't look much better. He rubbed his eyes. The coppery hair on his knuckles shone in the late-afternoon sunlight. "What do you think, Kitty?"

Kitty Keyes looked drawn; her face was powdery and her lipstick was cracking around the edges. "I don't know, either. This has been so . . ." She searched for a word, but all she came up with was ". . . much."

All I could say was "Yeah."

I had hung out on Puesta del Sol for a while, getting secondhand chunks and niblets of the story from some of the American neighbors. Apparently Felina's cleaning woman had arrived that morning, let herself into the house, straightened up the kitchen, got out the vacuum, went to plug it in, and found her employer's body stuffed behind the couch. Screaming, she had run out of the house, down the deck stairs, and onto the beach, where two local fishermen had come to her aid.

From there, the stories started to diverge. Some said the house had been robbed; others swore that it was a maniac on the loose. The cleaning woman had used *asalto*—the Spanish word for assault—but no one was quite sure if Felina had been raped. In any case, none of the neighbors had heard any noise, seen any cars, noticed any strangers in town. Except me, of course.

My press I.D. took off some of the heat, but I still got out of Via del Paraiso soon after that. All I needed was some paranoid busybody tipping off the Ensenada P.D. An interrogation by a Mexican cop—in a Mexican jail—wasn't my idea of fun. So I'd gone back to the Hotel del Toros, called Jocelyn and Danziger, got through the border check, and headed up the San Diego Freeway toward L.A.

"So, Sport. Where's the manuscript?" Danziger asked.

"I've got it."

"Great. I'll have Daria make a copy and go over it tonight."

I shifted in my chair, looking at the Jocelyn box. "Actually, I don't have it on me."

That was true; it was down in my trunk, hidden under the spare tire. Jocelyn had told me not to turn it over to Danziger under any circumstances. It was our only chance to keep the project alive.

Danziger grunted. "How is it?"

"Felina never showed it to me," said Kitty.

"I think it's what you want. Combined with the interview tapes, that is."

He nodded, pinching the bridge of his nose. "Let's sleep on it. I've got my lawyer talking to the Mexican police. When he gets some answers, maybe we can decide how to proceed. I don't want it to seem like we're profiteering off this tragedy."

I looked at the framed book covers on the walls and didn't say anything.

"Jack, who's your lawyer?" asked the Jocelyn box.

"Gilbert Françon at Dunne, Dunne, and Lambert."

More bad news. Dunne, Dunne, and Lambert was L.A.'s biggest entertainment law firm. Their hourly billable was more than I paid for rent in a month—*used* to pay. Françon was one of their hotshots, with a daughter at Marlborough and a wife on the Blue Ribbon board at the Music Center. If Danziger was inclined to invoke *force majeure* and drop the project, Jocelyn and I didn't have a chance against Gilbert Françon.

"Fine," said Jocelyn. "I just wanted to make it clear that my client is ready and willing to go on this project. You'll both be getting a fax to that effect in the morning. And you do want to go ahead with this, don't you, Kieran?"

Danziger and Kitty Keyes looked at me.

No, I wanted to say. *No, this is a project that turns my stomach. No, I can't turn a badly written memoir into a sizzling tell-all. No, even though I'm temporarily homeless and my bank account is running on fumes, I won't stoop to the level of—*

"Kieran?" said the Jocelyn box.

"Yeah," I said again. "Let's do it."

In the elevator, I offered to escort Kitty to her car. "That would be lovely, dear," she said tonelessly, offering a tired smile. "Your agent is very protective of you."

"I'm sorry if she seemed insensitive."

"Jocelyn was thinking of the book. Besides, that's what agents get paid for. To be unpleasant so our clients don't have to."

She gave me another tired smile as the doors slid open on P-2, and took my arm as we walked through the garage. Her heels clicked on the concrete. "I am sorry about Felina," I said. "Really."

"I was close to her, you know. Despite her past and her eccentricities, she was a good person. She had a spark."

Kitty stopped in front of a car and opened her bag. I'd envisioned her driving a Mary Kay–pink Cadillac convertible, so it was a disappointment to see that her car was a plain Mercedes, painted banker's-lamp green. She got out her keys and deactivated the alarm. The Mercedes gave off a metallic chirp.

"Can I drop you anywhere, dear?"

"No, I've still got my rental car."

"All right, then." I didn't move. "Did you have something you wanted to ask me?"

"You know Jack Danziger. What do you think the chances are . . ."

"Of the book getting done? Do you think you have enough information?"

"Well, I've got the manuscript, and the tapes." Not a lie.

Kitty appraised me shrewdly. Despite her dithery demeanor, this woman was no dummy. "And do you want to, dear?"

"Yes."

"Well, let me see what I can do, then." Kitty punched in a combination and opened her car door. She gave me another smile, and this one didn't look so weary. "The book will happen. One way or another. I promise."

It was seven-thirty by the time I got back to Claudia's. She wasn't there. Judging from the debris level, she'd barely been home since I left. By the time I took a cool shower and put my dirty clothes in a garbage bag for the cleaners, it was almost eight, and Claudia still wasn't home. I hadn't eaten since Denny's that morning, so I raided the refrigerator and came up with a container of coffee yogurt, a jar with olive water at the bottom, and some kind of leftovers in an old margarine tub. Grumbling, I called the House of Phuket and ordered in twenty-eight dollars' worth of Thai food. It was expensive, but . . . well . . . phuket.

When the phone rang a few minutes later, I assumed it was the delivery boy, lost somewhere, but it was Jack Danziger.

"The book's off, right? Well, nice working with you."

He laughed. "Hey, Sport. Don't jump to conclusions. I thought you'd want to know: I just got off the phone with Enrique Gustavo of the Mexican police."

"So what happened?"

"They think it was a simple case of robbery that got out of hand. The place was torn apart and some jewelry was missing. None of the neighbors noticed anything, but from what Gustavo told me, I gather that break-ins aren't uncommon down there."

I was telling him about Via del Paraiso, how the luxury was cheek-to-jowl with the poverty, when Claudia came in. Her hair was tied back in a purple bandanna, and there was fine plaster dust all over her shirt and shorts. The bags under her eyes were big enough for two weeks in Cancun. She dumped three sacks of food on the counter and disappeared into the bathroom.

"I've got a breakfast meeting tomorrow," said Jack. "But I'll be in touch with your agent sometime tomorrow, Sport."

"Thanks." I hung up, uneasy about something. Something about the conversation didn't sit right, and I couldn't figure out what it was. I opened one of the bags and took out a container of soup. The aromas of lemongrass and galangal permeated the room like steam.

"You off?" Claudia yelled.

"Yeah. Thanks for getting the food."

"I met the delivery boy downstairs. You owe me fourteen bucks." The shower went on with a shudder of pipes. "So when'd you get back?"

"A couple of hours ago."

"I thought you were there through the weekend. . . . Why can't I get any hot water?"

"What?"

"Did everything go okay?"

"I'll tell you later. Why don't you take a shower and I'll get the food set up?"

"I can't hear you," she yelled. "I'm in the shower."

The kitchen table was still covered with my unpacked cardboard boxes. I laid a tablecloth on the floor, set two places, and was spooning green beans over rice when Claudia came out of the bathroom, hair wet and wearing a Saints jersey. She pecked me on the cheek, and I took her in my arms for a hug, but she wriggled away.

"Eat first," she said. "Kiss later."

While we ate, she told me all the latest complications: the discovery of termites in one of the supporting columns, the contractor who had vanished and wasn't returning messages. I pinched lime and sprinkled peanuts on my noodles, asking questions in the right places. When she was done, I told her an abbreviated version of my adventures with Felina. "That was Danziger on the phone when you came in. His lawyer talked to the cops down there."

"So what happened?" Claudia walked over to the fridge. "You want a beer?"

"Sure . . . They think it was a break-in gone wrong. There's something weird about—" I looked at the beer Claudia handed me. "Dixie?"

"My parents sent a care package. Craw-Tator chips, cane root beer, everything. My mother put in a note and said they're coming out for the grand opening of Canem."

"Oh. Good."

Claudia's parents had always treated me cordially, considering my precarious financial and social situation. Both of them came from old New Orleans families; it was a merger as much as a marriage. I liked the Doctors Dubuisson, but I wasn't quite sure what they thought about me.

"Lydia's coming, too," Claudia continued. "She and Charlie split up a couple of weeks ago."

"What happened?"

"No one's clear on it. You know Lydia."

Lydia was Claudia's older sister by two years. They shared facial features, but where Claudia was all angles and ambition, Lydia was pure curves and languor. She was a travel agent, but she also worked part-time as a "plus-size" model in department store fashion shows, modeling sixteens with a panache that no anorexic runway rat could match. I liked Lydia, but her laissez-faire attitude toward child rearing made me nervous. Her motto was "If they're not dead at the end of the day, I've done my job."

Claudia took another bite of curry and washed it down with Dixie. "So what's going to happen with the book?"

"I'm still not sure. I could paste something together. Even with padding, though, I'm not sure it's enough for a whole book. And Danziger's backpedaling." I explained *force majeure* to

Claudia. "The ball's in his court, and he's got Dunne, Dunne, and Lambert to back him up."

"So if he decides to pull out, you're screwed."

"Pretty much." I killed the Dixie and started to clear away the remains of the dinner. "Listen, Claude, I'm sorry. I'll get out of here soon. Somehow. I promise."

"Don't worry about it. Something will happen. It always does." Claudia got up and stretched. "Right now I'm too tired to think about it, and I've got to be back at Canem at seven in the morning."

"Go to bed. I'll clean up."

"Just dump it in the sink, Kieran. You can take care of it to-morrow." She started toward the bedroom and banged her shin on a packing box. "Ow. Dammit."

"I'll get that cleared away tomorrow," I mumbled.

Claudia shot me a look that told me what she thought of my promises these days.

In bed, she curled into me spoon-fashion and was asleep in a minute. I, on the other hand, was too exhausted for sleep. Tired but wired. And I wasn't sure what was weighing on my mind—Felina's death, the fate of the book project, or Claudia and me.

How the hell am I going to save this project?

How could Felina afford that beach house, anyway?

Under my arm, Claudia shifted, pressing herself into my chest. Her breath came heavy.

Once, this position would have built into slow kisses, hands all over each other, rummaging in my old gym bag for condoms and lubricant. Since I'd moved in with Claude, any passion was gone between us. Even our arguments had dribbled away into inconsequence, as if none of it mattered anymore.

Claude, what's happened to us?

She was gone when I woke up in the morning. The backdrop of sky over the Pacific Ocean was roiling, black as poison. The one clean pair of 501s I found took a little extra tugging to get them over my hips. Wonderful. Just past my thirtieth birthday, and soon I'd be shopping for "relaxed fit" jeans. The first stop on the long downhill slide to Dentu-Creme and Depends.

Claudia had left a carafe of French roast, and I scared up a couple pieces of toast, smearing them with cream cheese. Not bad; nine in the morning, and I already had two food groups out of the way. Three, if you count coffee.

The morning paper didn't have anything on Felina's death. I went on to Ann Landers and Metro, relieved.

Rain began to fall, a restless sound. I turned on the lamps in the living room, making it cozy as a ship's cabin. I got out my laptop and the Felina tapes and started transcribing.

At twelve-thirty, thoroughly discouraged, I took a break for lunch. There were tidbits here and there—some juicy stuff about Vernon Ash and the Hollywood drug scene, Dick and Betty Mann's marriage—but it still felt more like an article than a book. If only I had one more day with Felina, I might have been able to stitch together a workable manuscript, but nothing short of a channeler could make Felina available for rewrites.

Crap. I put last night's leftovers into the microwave and watched them spin in the little window.

The phone rang.

"Kieran?" It was Jack Danziger. I pictured him leaning back in an ergonomic executive chair, talking into one of the little operator headsets that all the Hollywood types used. "How's it going?"

"Fine. Just transcribing Felina's tapes."

"You think there's enough there for a book?"

"Sure," I lied. The two primary rules of Hollywood deal-making are "Anything's possible" and "Tell them what they want to hear."

"Good. I'll be talking to Jocelyn in a day or two, as soon as I figure out what's going on. Listen, Sport; I had a call from Frank Grassley a few minutes ago."

Frank Grassley used to be a local TV reporter in Los Angeles, a town where journalism skills were never as important as really good hair. Frank had excellent hair. A few months back, Frank had left the *Eyewitless News* beat to become an "investigative reporter" for *Hollywood Today!*, an entertainment show that sucked up to the stars. Frank and I had crossed paths a few times over the years, never with pleasant results.

"He's doing a story on Felina. He wanted an interview," Danziger said grimly. "I told him no."

"Good. Grassley's a sleaze."

"I know. But get this: Then he asked for your phone number."

"My . . . how did he get my name?"

"I don't know. You're a reporter. How do you people get your information?"

"Frank Grassley isn't a reporter. He's a two-hundred-dollar coiffure with a microphone."

"Of course I didn't give it to him." I heard a beep. "I've got to take that. Listen, he left a number in case you want to call him. You want it?"

"No. Thanks, Jack."

Shit. I found the TV listings from the morning paper. *Hollywood Today!* came on at six-thirty, right after the local news. With a little luck, it would be a busy news day and the Felina story wouldn't merit more than a footnote. With a little luck . . .

A little luck was a lot to ask for.

I tried to go back to work, but Danziger's call was eating at me. What the hell could Frank Grassley want? At one-thirty I gave up and headed for downtown. I needed to do some research.

I parked in the Second Street garage and jaywalked over to the paper, feeling vaguely like a shoplifter returning to the scene of the crime. But the guard in the lobby said hello as always, giving my ID badge the most cursory of glances, and no alarm bells went off when I got on the elevator.

Sally's pod was in the back of the fourth-floor bullpens, a tiny cubicle dominated by teetering stacks of reference books, several weeks' worth of old dummies, and her prized Wayne Gretsky jersey. Sitting in the middle of it all was a giant Coyote monitor that bathed the full catastrophe in a sickly green light. Sally was typing away like a madwoman, oblivious.

"I've been a subscriber for sixty years, and I'm sick and tired of the hidden Satanic messages in *The Family Circus*," I said.

Without missing a keystroke, Sally waved at a nearby chair. Shut up and sit down.

Like every other company in America, the paper was undergoing what management referred to as cutbacks, buyouts, and "right-sizing." Employees had several other words for it, none of them suitable for a family newspaper. The cutback was a companywide constriction, but it had hit no other section harder than the one for which Sally and I worked. There would always be room for sports and business, but the "soft" pages such as features were taking a big hit.

Sally finally stopped typing and pressed her hands together, trying to ease the carpal tunnel—reporter's arthritis—in her wrists. Her hair needed a trim, and she'd put on a few pounds.

"Busy?" I said brightly.

She tossed me that day's section. "There's less and less of us, and it just keeps getting smaller and smaller."

"Are you trying to tell me something?"

Sally didn't react.

"What? Have you heard something? Am I not coming back?"

"I don't know, Kieran, honestly." She dropped her voice. "I don't know if there's going to be a section to come back to. It's just cafeteria chatter at this point, but there's talk about folding the section unless advertising picks up."

"I'm sure you'd be okay. They'd move you to Metro or something."

"I doubt it. I've been here twenty-seven years, Kieran. With what I'm making, they could hire three kids straight out of J-school." She rubbed her wrists. "I don't want to think about it. What are you doing here?"

"I need to use the library."

"You might as well. No one else is." She swiveled and began typing again.

"Call me when you get a minute. I'll take you to coffee."

She nodded distractedly.

Up in the library, I sat down in front of the supercomputer we called the Beast. It was really a hypersophisticated web crawler; type in a name, a place, a string of words, and some lightning-fast computer chip would comb the electronic catacombs for matches. It felt good to lose myself in research and forget the conversation with Sally. If the section folded, my job prospects would be reduced to asking if people wanted fries with that.

I typed in "Felina Lopez" and "Vernon Ash." The hits started piling up on my screen in a bright green scroll—first a dozen, then two, then more.

Two hits down, I found a long story that summarized the Ash case. The story had broken during a particularly slow, hot summer, and the combination of Hollywood, hookers, drug dealing, and melodramatic testimony had captivated the L.A. media until fall.

Ash had been a slickie—not a streetcorner crack peddler, but a guy who had serviced some big names in the movie, television, and music industries. A whippet-thin pretty boy, Ash had a penchant for Italian suits, celebrity parties, and flashy girlfriends like Felina Lopez. He was too tempting a target for the then-D.A., whose tenure had been marred by a series of high-profile courtroom losses. By the time *voir dire* started, there was a semipermanent media camp outside the Santa Monica courthouse.

In Los Angeles, trials are run like Hollywood productions. By the third week, *People v. Ash* was shaping up as a flop. Interest was waning. Then Felina took the stand.

Just as Fawn Hall perked up the Iran-contra hearings, Felina got the Ash case back on top of the evening news. The press zeroed in on the beautiful dark blonde with the long legs, and the very first question—"Have you ever been a prostitute?"—was the clincher. Ash would probably have been sent away even without her testimony, but Felina's information, provided under immunity, was the clincher.

When it was over, Felina went to Mexico, Ash got a few years in a low-security prison with satellite TV, and the D.A. won reelection. A happy ending for everyone.

Claudia came home at six to watch. At 6:25, we popped a tape in the VCR and tuned in the last of the local news, just in time to catch a cutesy human-interest story about a German shepherd that was nursing a litter of motherless piglets. The weather goofball made a stupid joke, everyone laughed, and they segued into the familiar theme song of *Hollywood Today!*

Mary Lasater, the host, was sitting behind her Plexiglas desk with a smile that looked wheatpasted on her face. Mary had a few miles on her odometer, but she was still as slappably perky as ever. The music ended and the opening graphic appeared behind her: a sexy photo of a young Felina. Bright red lettering spelled out the title BUTCHERED BEAUTY.

"Oh, brother," said Claudia.

"Several years ago, Felina Lopez was living the high life," said Mary Lasater. "As a high-priced Hollywood call girl, she hobnobbed with the rich and famous. Four years ago, she left Tinseltown after turning state's evidence on Vernon Ash, the drug dealer to the stars, and moved to Mexico to begin a new life. That life came to a tragic end yesterday when Felina Lopez was found murdered in her beach mansion. For the story, we go to Ensenada, Mexico, and Frank Grassley."

Grassley was walking on the beach in a polo shirt. He wore a grim look on his face and a pair of four-hundred-dollar leather espadrilles on his feet.

"That's right, Mary. Felina Lopez lived in the house you see behind me. Mexican police are calling her murder a case of robbery gone wrong, but *Hollywood Today!* has learned of another possible motive. Recently, Felina Lopez had signed a contract to write the story of her life—a book that was going to detonate like a bomb in Hollywood."

"Shit," I mumbled.

The image switched to a biographical montage underscored with Donna Summer's "Bad Girls." Lots of file footage from Hollywood parties past, a shot of Felina leaving the L.A. county courthouse during the Ash trial, and finally—sad music swelling—grainy video of the Mexican cops removing the body bag from Felina's house.

Back to Frank Grassley, who was now in suit and tie, sitting in a busy newsroom. It was a lie; the real *Hollywood Today!* "newsroom" looked like a basement where they'd conduct telephone scams. In reality, Grassley was sitting in front of a blue screen with footage of a phony newsroom superimposed behind him. But it sure looked real. "A robbery gone wrong?" he repeated. "Or . . . something more sinister?

"*Hollywood Today!* has learned exclusively that Felina Lopez was getting ready to publish a memoir of her experiences in Tinseltown. And that the centerpiece of this book was going to be her relationship with the late Dick Mann." An ominous music sting over a picture of Dick and Betty Bradford Mann at the Emmys. "Felina Lopez and Dick Mann were lovers, according to one woman who knew them both—a woman who also worked as a call girl. We've disguised her identity here."

No duh. The woman on the screen wore a wig, sunglasses, and was photographed entirely in shadow. A caption read "MISSY": FORMER HOLLYWOOD PROSTITUTE.

"Felina and Dick were dating for almost a year," said the woman. Her voice had been electronically altered. She sounded like she'd been sucking helium underwater.

"How did they meet?" Grassley asked from offscreen. From the odd break between the statement and the question, I guessed that the interview had actually been done by some anonymous producer with Grassley dubbing in his questions later. Just another bit of fudging with the facts.

"He started as a client of the agency where we both worked."

"And you're telling me that their relationship developed from a prostitute and her client to something more."

"I always had that impression. Felina talked about him all the time."

"But he was married. To Betty Bradford Mann." A quick cutaway to a telephoto shot of the actress leaving her husband's funeral.

"He was married. Felina knew it. We all did."

Frank put on a stern face. "Missy—do you think Felina Lopez's tragic death might have something to do with this book she was planning to write?"

"I don't know."

Back to Via del Paraiso, where Frank Grassley stood on the beach like a Ken doll. "There you have it, Mary. We tried to reach Betty Bradford Mann for comment, but she was unavailable. We also tried to reach this man—"

"Kieran!" yelped Claudia.

It was a picture of me.

Some freelance video photographer—*videorazzi* was the word—had caught me standing in front of a buffet table. They say the camera puts on fifteen pounds, but here it looked more like thirty. In the footage, I was gnawing on a spring roll like a mook.

"This is Kieran O'Connor, a former entertainment columnist who was ghostwriting the project with Felina Lopez. We tried all day to contact Mr. O'Connor, but, Mary . . ." Frank took a pause that was not only pregnant but ready to deliver. "He couldn't be located."

Mary Lasater sucked in the skin below her cheek implants. "I hope he's okay."

"We all do," said Frank Grassley, "and we'll keep trying to locate him. In the meantime, we'll have Part Two of our exclusive interview with Missy tomorrow."

I aimed the remote like a gun and zapped the TV. The image died.

"Kieran, they made it sound like you'd gotten kidnapped or gone into hiding!"

"It's just something Frank Grassley would pull. I wouldn't return his call and he's not smart enough to find me, so he gets even by making it sound like a case for the FBI."

Claudia sighed. "So you think the book is off?"

"I don't know, Claude. I just don't know."

Claudia went back to the shop about eight and I did a couple loads of clothes. No matter how little or how much you bring on a trip, all your clothes come back dirty. After a long, not particularly relaxing bath, all I could find to wear was a T-shirt and a pair of Halloween boxers patterned with pumpkins.

I poured myself a glass of wine and laid down on the bed to read the transcripts, listening to the soft drizzle on the roof. Before long, I had dozed off.

The phone woke me.

My head jerked up from the drool-spotted pillow. Eleven o'-clock. I heard the machine pick up, and then a dial tone. Whoever was calling had hung up.

I laid down again, uneasy. Claudia would have left a message. My guess was Frank Grassley.

Twice more during the night the phone rang, but I didn't get up to answer it. The second time was at one-fifteen, and Claudia still wasn't home.

5

"KIERNAN O'CONNOR?"

The woman on Claudia's stoop couldn't have been more than twenty-three, with mink-black hair and expensive department store makeup all over her pretty face.

"Are you Kiernan?"

"Kieran," I corrected her reflexively, leaning against the door frame. It wasn't even eight o'clock, and I'd been awake all of forty-five seconds.

"Kieran. I'm sorry. I'm Shelly Nguyen." She slipped me a business card that read SHELLY NGUYEN • SEGMENT PRODUCER • HEADLINE JOURNAL. Under it was a mini-directory of contact information: office, home, mobile, fax, E-mail. This was a woman who couldn't afford to be out of touch for a single minute. "I hope I didn't wake you up."

" 'S okay. I was just sleeping."

"Right. Hey, you're funny. I was just working on a story? About the Felina Lopez case? And I'd love to interview you."

"When?" I was still dopey.

"Now." She pointed down at the curb, where a black stretch limousine was waiting.

Suddenly it all made sense. This was a standard maneuver that the tabloid-TV shows used when they were trying to get an interview out of a noncelebrity: show up at the house with a shiny black limo and treat 'em like a star.

"You could have skipped the car," I said. "I'm not a dismissed juror. Or the sole survivor of an air disaster."

"I know," said Shelly Nguyen. "You're a writer, and a good one. Of course, we'd want to pay you for your time and insights." She handed me an envelope. I opened it.

Inside was a bank draft made payable to Kiernan O'Connor.

"Okay," I said after a brief pause. "I'll do it. On the condition that you answer me one thing."

"What?"

"How did you find me?"

Shelly Nguyen smiled. "We have our ways."

"I know. I'm a reporter, too. But how'd you get the address where I was staying?"

Her smile flickered. "I don't know. I didn't get it myself. My assistant did."

"Tell me. I don't care. I'm just curious."

"It could have been the phone book, or voter registration rolls."

"Nope. My place was destroyed during the earthquake. And this isn't my permanent residence."

"Maybe the DMV."

"No," I said. "The Rebecca Schaeffer law."

"Hmm?" Her head looked up from her clipboard.

"Not the DMV. You might be too young to remember, but a few years ago there was a young actress who got murdered.

The guy got her address from the DMV. They passed a law in the California legislature, and now you can't get home addresses from the DMV. Legally, at least."

Something in the air between us shifted. Shelly Nguyen had the business suit and the cashier's check, but it was me, in my T-shirt and Halloween boxers, who had control of the situation.

"So come on, Shelly," I said. "Just tell me and I'll get dressed and go with you."

Shelly rolled her eyes. She took a piece of paper from her clipboard and handed it to me.

It was a Xerox of my last pay stub from the newspaper, which had Claudia's address printed right under the pay-to line.

Someone at my own paper had ratted me out. For their own *Headline Journal* bank draft, no doubt.

"Well, Shelly, I guess that makes us both liars."

"Huh?" She was still smiling.

I smiled back and handed her the bank draft. "You and *Headline Journal* can go fuck yourselves."

And then I slammed the door in Shelly Nguyen's face.

"They think I know something!" I was crouched on the living room floor, my back to the wall.

"Get out of there. Go stay somewhere else."

"You're not listening! I can't even go outside to get the paper, Jocelyn!"

"Calm down. Try to look at the positive side. The tabloids are saying that Felina got murdered over what she intended to write. And Danziger's decided to go ahead with the book."

"Of course he has! Everyone in this city wants the story!"

"Calm down, Kieran, and listen." Jocelyn had on her soothing voice, the aural equivalent of honey and Prozac. "There won't be any extra money up front. He does have a signed contract, but you should do very well on the back end. But you have to work fast."

"How can I work like this? I'm sitting on the floor right now because they're shooting through my—"

"Shooting?"

"Not with an Uzi. With a six-hundred-millimeter lens!"

I crawled to the window and peeked out the blind. Sometime during the morning, my address had gotten out. Down on Fourteenth Street, three news vans were parked outside, their satellite dishes and phallic antennas outlined against the trees. Crews were sitting placidly on the curbs, like birds in a Hitchcock movie. One of the neighbors must have called the cops, because there was a Santa Monica police cruiser down there, too, making sure the news crews stayed on public property. I didn't have much time before one of the crews would find a neighbor who would gladly take a hundred-dollar bill in exchange for letting the stalkerazzi into their living room to point a video camera at my window.

Claudia's call-waiting clicked in. "Ignore that, Kieran. Now listen. Get out of there any way you can, Peaches. Get a hotel room or go stay with a friend. As soon as you're safe, call me and let me know where you are."

The phone started ringing again the second I broke the connection.

I tossed my duffel out the bedroom window. It landed with a squish in the still-wet ground. The drop was twelve feet or so.

I breathed deeply, made sure my laptop was strapped securely to my back, relaxed my knees, and dropped after it. Ouch. I laid in the dichondra, trying to catch my breath and still my heart. Biscuit, the neighbors' Jack Russell terrier, came over and sniffed me without any particular interest, as if I dropped into his backyard every morning.

Claudia was waiting for me in the supermarket parking lot at Fourteenth and Wilshire. Her sunglasses hid her eyes, and I couldn't read her face.

"Thanks, Claude."

She started the car and we merged with the noontime traffic on Wilshire. "So where are we going?"

"There's some cheap motels over on Pico. But I need to go to the ATM first."

After a minute, she said, "I drove past the house. What have you stepped in, Kieran?"

"A pile of Biscuit's shit."

She reached over and punched a cassette into the dash, and the sad, sweet voices of Lyle Lovett and Shawn Colvin came out of the back speaker. I looked at Claudia's hand. There was a white clayish material under the nails, and her second finger was bare.

"Where's your ring?"

"I took it off this morning when I was grouting the bathroom."

"You could have put it back on," I said after a moment.

"I just forgot."

I looked out the window. A homeless crone was inching her way up the sidewalk, towing a caravan of shopping carts roped together with knotted plastic bags. "Did you really forget?"

"Oh, Kieran." Claudia's voice was exhausted. "There's enough going on. Drop the paranoia."

Claudia pulled into the Wind & Sea, an anonymous little fleabag motel with a neon schooner on the roof and a battered marquee that advertised W KLY RATS • FREE L CAL CAL S • COL R TV. I sat in the car while Claudia used her Visa to book me a room for a week. She had already driven away by the time I got the rusty key in the door marked 17.

I unpacked my bag into a pressboard drawer and turned on the A/C. A trickle of air dribbled out of the ceiling, a wheezy wisp that could only be described as luke-cold. The room had a bed with a ratty chenille spread, a television on a swivel pole, and chocolate hi-lo carpeting that crunched under my sneakers. It smelled like the inside of a dryer. I turned down the bed and found something brown on my pillow.

It wasn't a mint.

Well, I thought, at least I've got FREE L CAL CAL S.

Information didn't turn up any Sloan Bakers in the metro area. Next I tried a buddy of mine who worked for the phone company. We had a deal: free screening passes in exchange for access to what he called the "unlistings."

Still no Sloans in 310, 213, or 818, but there were three unlisted S. Bakers, one in each area code. I jotted down the numbers, for the first time feeling slimy about it. Before, using my pal at the phone company had felt like just another arrow in a well-connected reporter's quiver. Now it seemed something a sleaze would do.

What the hell. I dialed the 310 S. Baker. A woman picked up.

"Sloan?" I said cheerfully. Rule one: Disarm them. An unknown voice on the phone saying "I'm looking for Sloan Baker" would get anyone's guard up.

"You've got the wrong number." Click.

From the sound of it, 213 S. Baker was an elderly black woman with a hearing problem. And 818 S. Baker was an answering machine: Steve and Stephanie couldn't come to the phone right now, but I got to hear their toddler's rendition of "Good Morning Starshine." I made a vomiting noise at the sound of the beep and hung up.

Strike three and out. I sighed and got out my long-distance calling card.

The *Celeb* offices were in Cocoa Beach, Florida. A receptionist explained that Gina Guglielmelli was a staff writer in the L.A. bureau and gave me Gina's extension. She picked up on the first ring. I explained who I was and why I was calling. She chuckled.

"O'Connor, you wouldn't give away your sources," she said. "Why should I?"

"I'm not asking you to betray a source. I just want to talk to 'Desiree.' Obviously she's willing to talk. And I'm not your competition. Can't you just pass my number on to her and let her make the decision?"

There was a long pause. "Let me ask you something," Gina finally said. "Would you ask the same thing of me if I worked for *The New York Times*?"

". . . No."

"O'Connor, I'm a reporter. Oh, I know that you people in the so-called legit media think we're all a bunch of ambulance chasers and gutter crawlers, but I have standards the same way you do. Higher, probably. I double-check and triple-check my sources."

"I'm sure you do, but—"

"But nothing. You want my c.v.? I went to Yale and the Columbia School of Journalism. Did you?"

I didn't say anything.

"Now tell me again why you expect me to put you in touch with a source I cultivated."

"That you paid for, you mean."

"Like you don't. Like you've never taken a source to lunch, or a Kings game, or done all kinds of favors for them."

"I have never taken a source to a Kings game."

"A screening, whatever. Can you tell me you've never done that?"

"Okay," I said tiredly. "You win. Sorry I bothered you."

"The world's changed, O'Connor. What's news has changed." She laughed. "And you legitimate types are still playing catch-up. I love it."

Gina Guglielmelli was still laughing as she slammed down the phone.

Red numerals on the bedside clock read 2:17. The glow from the laptop and the yellow sulphur lights in the parking lot gave the room a radioactive look. I took off my glasses and rubbed my aching eyes. Carpal tunnel was beginning to twinge through my fingers.

The last Felina tape had just clicked to a stop. It wasn't enough. Face it, I wasn't Barbara Walters. I wasn't even Gina

Guglielmelli. The only thing to do was get some sleep, dump the facts into Jocelyn's lap, and let her sort them out and break the news to Jack Danziger. Right now I was too tired to think about it.

The phone rang: once, then twice. I checked the clock again: 2:18 A.M.

A third ring.

Jocelyn still didn't know where I was staying. Could the press jackals have tracked me down to the Wind & Sea? We'd paid for the room with Claudia's credit card, and the desk clerk hadn't seen me check in. It was probably Claudia.

The phone rang a fourth time. I took a chance and picked it up.

"Hello?"

"You going ahead with the book?"

"What?"

"I said, you going ahead with the book?"

It was a man's voice. Not threatening, just deep and very, very self-assured.

"Who is this?"

No answer.

"How did you find me?"

"Think twice, buddy. Think twice."

The line went dead.

I sat on the edge of the bed with the receiver in my hand. The room glowed yellow.

After stepping out of the Jacuzzi, I stood on a bath mat that oozed up around my toes and reached for the woolly robe by the tub. The towel rack turned out to be heated. It was like putting on a feverish sheep.

I had been at the Beverly Hillshire for eight hours and I was enjoying every pig minute. The difference between writing a low-key cheesy tell-all and a high-profile cheesy tell-all was as big as the difference between—well, the Wind & Sea and the Beverly Hillshire Hotel.

I'd been in this suite once before, to interview a romance novel cover stud whose chest implants and steroid injections had given him a truly alarming pair of he-boobs. This time it was all mine: the berber carpets, the Porthault linens, the projection TV, the data and fax ports that bristled from every outlet, and the charming verdigris balcony overlooking the intersection of Wilshire and Rodeo. The room managed to be both luxe and high-tech, like a decorating collaboration between Jackie Collins and Bill Gates.

And—most important—it was all paid for by Jack Danziger.

By the time I talked to Jocelyn, I had calmed down to the point where the sound of a car pulling into the Wind & Sea parking lot didn't have me ready to lock myself in the bathroom. Jocelyn, on the other hand, was horrified. By eight-thirty, Kitty Keyes had shown up in her Mercedes to ferry me over to the Beverly Hillshire in cheerful style. Either she was as ditzy as she looked or death threats just came with the territory in her line of work.

I'd spent the morning napping and trying to set up interviews, with little success either way. The top of the list—and the longest shot—was Dick Mann's widow, Betty Bradford

Mann. Her press agent, Susan D'Andrea, guarded her clients in the same relaxed way that Nancy guarded Ronnie in the White House. Apparently D'Andrea had been deluged with requests for interviews; I spoke to some D-level assistant who told me to fax over a formal interview request. Translation: Buzz off.

Kitty Keyes had spirited up a beeper number for Sloan Baker, and I'd got a number for Vernon Ash through another reporter at the paper. I'd left messages for both, but neither had called back. The only response I'd had was from the Ensenada police, who faxed me back a press release on Felina's murder and a polite refusal to discuss the matter further. The fax told me that a search of the house revealed that valuables were taken. The cops' official take on it was a tragedy, a robbery gone wrong. Even if it wasn't, I was sure the police would cover it up for fear of scaring off the wealthy Americans in the neighborhood. A crazed killer would have the same effect on Via del Paraiso that the shark did in *Jaws*.

The phone rang. One of the perks in the suite was an unlisted phone that didn't go through the hotel switchboard. Management changed the number after each guest checked out.

"I'm returning a call left on my beeper. Who's calling, please?" She was aiming for a professional woman's voice, but a certain lazy nasality sneaked through on "beeper" and "please." A Valley doll—fer sure, fer sure.

"My name's Kieran O'Connor. I wanted to know if we could get together—"

"I don't know how you got this number, but you'll have to go through my agency," she interrupted.

"No, Sloan," I told her dryly, "that's not the kind of hour I want to spend."

Smooth Moo was a juice bar and New Age soda fountain adjoining Le Sweat, a particularly overpriced fitness palace on La Cienega. I pulled into the parking lot of Le Sweat and gave my keys to the valet. People in L.A. are nuts. They'll spend an hour on a StairMaster, but they won't walk fifty feet from their car to the gym.

One whole wall of Smooth Moo was glass, giving patrons a good view of the beautiful people as they crunched and burned and flexed and abbed their way to Aryan perfection. Taken individually, all the women were gorgeous, but in aggregate they blended into a boring, homogenous whole. I couldn't imagine myself having a conversation with any of them, much less a relationship. That's what I liked about Claudia. She worked out at the YWCA.

At Smooth Moo, the milkshakes were called smoothies and started at eight bucks apiece. There was also a bewildering list of optional mix-ins: bee pollen, acidophilus, protein powder, brewer's yeast. I chose the P-Nutty Pow—a concoction of peanut butter, bananas, and honey—just because it looked like the least healthy thing on the menu.

While I waited for Sloan, I sipped my P-Nutty Pow and watched the gym Barbies. Each of the high-tech stationary bikes was occupied by a blonde reading a script. They couldn't all be actresses. Maybe Le Sweat handed out old scripts at the reception desk, like getting a copy of *Newsweek* at the dentist's.

A woman walked in through the street entrance, and I almost choked on my P-Nutty Pow.

It was Felina.

No. On second glance, this woman was younger, maybe thirty. Still, the resemblance was striking. From a distance, they could have been, if not sisters, then maybe a star and her stunt double.

I tried to make some small talk—lay a little verbal grease before the grilling began—but Sloan wasn't much interested. She ordered a drink called And Tofu, Too and brushed the hair out of her eyes. Up close, the resemblance started to fall apart. The retroussé nose was too obviously a rhinoplasty, and the streaks in her hair were Clairol instead of chlorine. Small differences, but they added up to the difference between a beauty queen and first runner-up.

"Okay. I'm here," Sloan said, as if the sentence itself was an effort. "Now what do you want from me?"

I got out my tape recorder. "You mind if I—"

"Put that away. I'm not giving you any interview."

"It's not an interview. I'd just like you to answer a few questions."

"Forget it. I'm not going to rat anyone out."

"Without getting paid for it, you mean?"

She folded her arms and glared. "What does that—"

"Get off it, Sloan. You sold your Dick Mann story to *Celeb* and to *Headline Journal.*"

"I don't know what you're talking about."

"Come on, *Desiree.*"

"You come on. Who do you think you are, Woodward and Birdstein or something? It's no secret that Dick Mann hired sex workers. It doesn't mean I ever slept with him."

Sex worker, I guessed, was the union term for hooker, like *maintenance engineer* for janitor. It sounded so much nicer than *ho* or *hoochie*.

"Everyone in town knew that Dick Mann liked hookers," she continued. "Hey, I've got some other big scoops for you. Rock Hudson was a fag. And Joan Crawford smacked her kids."

"Felina named you."

Sloan's tofu shake arrived. She poked at it with the straw, considering. "Okay. So say I've got some information on Dick Mann. Why should I give it to you for free? If it's all that valuable, I could write my own story."

"You could. But I've got a book contract."

"Who cares? I'm not saying it's true, and I'm not saying it's not true. She's dead. So is he. And so is this story." Sloan stood up. "Thanks for the smoothie."

"Sloan. Sit."

"I don't let men tell me what to do."

"So stand up. But hear this. I have Felina, on tape, telling me that not only did you have sex with Dick Mann, but that you sold him out to the tabs. If it comes out that you've been double-dealing your clients to the tabs, every decent agency in town will drop you."

"You don't know what you're talking about."

"Get real! You think men pay those agencies thousands of dollars because you're so goddamn good in the sack? They're buying your silence, Sloan. And you've been selling them out. If you want a reason you should talk to me, how about this one: I could ruin your career."

Her face went hot, and the muscles in her jaw vibrated like

a tuning fork. For a moment, I thought she might throw her smoothie in my face.

"Sit down, Sloan. Let's talk."

She thought about it. And she sat.

"About four years ago this guy who was a reporter for *Celeb* called me one night. On my unlisted phone. He offered me big money. Plus more, if they ran a story."

"Wait a minute. What do you mean, *if* they ran a story?"

"They weren't looking for a big story. They just wanted to make some new friends."

"Friends?"

"Friends . . . It's a term the tabs use for somebody who co-operates with them."

"You mean they wanted some names for blackmail."

"Not blackmail. They wouldn't ask for money. But the tabs might use them for access."

"Access to what?"

"Well—like, Dick was a friend of *Celeb*. They had files on him. So once or twice a year, he'd give them an exclusive interview. He did one on how to keep a happy marriage in Hollywood. When he and Betty adopted their son, *Celeb* got rights to the photos. That's what a friend does. Both sides cooperate and everybody's happy."

Sloan sighed. "We kept talking, and he said that I could make extra money by feeding him items."

"On people you slept with?"

"No. I went out to restaurants and clubs a lot. Just for letting him know who was there and who they were with, he'd send me a check."

That sounded authentic to me. The tabloids had a vast network of stringers in service positions: waiters, hairdressers, busboys, valets, shop clerks. If Heather Locklear dropped three thousand dollars on a jogging outfit, somebody, somewhere, would call the tabs.

"About a month later," she continued, "I was at this restaurant in Malibu with a client, and I saw this movie star out with some woman who wasn't his wife. So I remembered the guy at *Celeb*. I called him, and he sent me a check for a thousand dollars. A thousand dollars for one phone call. And that was how it started."

"So you started calling him with tidbits on your clients."

"I *never* did that. You're not listening," Sloan said, aggrieved. "Just innocent stuff. Public stuff. So-and-so was drunk at such-and-such a party. That kind of thing."

"The kind of thing that couldn't be traced back to you."

She shrugged. "I thought it was harmless. Until."

"Until what?"

"Until Dick died." She nibbled at her nail, leaving tooth marks in the French manicure. "My contact called and said he had proof that I'd slept with Dick. Once you die, you're not a friend anymore, you know what I mean? Anyway, I told him I didn't want to talk about it."

"And he threatened you."

"Not threatened, really. But he let me know he had copies of all the checks they'd sent me over the years. If I didn't cooperate, he'd spread it around that I was a source. Like *you* want to do," she added pitifully.

I wasn't moved. "They made you into a friend. Isn't that ironic."

"Whatever. So I went ahead and did the interview. And then *Headline Journal* called. That bastard at *Celeb* sold me out to them, too."

"What did you expect, Sloan? There's no loyalty with the tabs. If there's a story at stake, you're going to be expendable."

There was a dot of smoothie on the table, and she dragged her finger through it pensively. "So are you gonna rat me out, too?"

"I doubt it."

"Good." She pushed back her chair. "Are we done?"

"Hardly. We haven't even started." I got out my microcassette. "I know where you're coming from, and now you're going to give me an interview."

She stared at me, dumbfounded. "Are you telling me that if I don't talk to you, you're . . . Are you trying to blackmail me?"

"No. I'm trying to get an interview."

"Well, chuck you, Farley, 'cause I don't have anything to say."

"Why? Because I'm not gonna cut you a check?"

"No. Because you're scum. I thought you people in the so-called legitimate press were supposed to be so high and mighty. You're a hypocrite. You're no better than Leo Lazarnick."

"Hey. You don't compare me to Lazarnick, and I won't compare you to a ten-dollar crack whore on Hollywood Boulevard. Got it, lady?"

"Why not? He uses a camera, you use a pen. You both make your living ruining other people's lives." She stood up, furious. "Go talk to Leo and leave me alone. He knew Felina a lot better than I ever did."

She wiggled her way out of Smooth Moo, earning a few admiring glances from a table of abdominized dudes near the door.

I took a long slow draught of my P-Nutty Pow.

There are several castes of photographers in Hollywood. At the top are the ones hired by the event organizers, classy types who are indistinguishable from the other guests except for the cameras around their necks. Next are the "pack" photogs, the ones you see on TV standing outside strobing arrivals. Below them are the scumbums. They spy on people with telephoto lenses or ambush their prey, hoping for that angry reaction or raised middle finger that can be sold to the tabs for big bucks. They're at the bottom of the Fuji food chain.

Leo Lazarnick, however, was *sui generis*. His nickname was the Nazi Paparazzi. Scourge of the rich and famous, he hid in Dumpsters at rehab centers and crashed funerals with a micro-camera hidden in his tie. It had made him a fortune. You could say Leo Lazarnick was a well-known Hollywood photographer, sort of, but that would be like describing Jeffrey Dahmer as a well-known Milwaukee gourmet.

How could the Nazi Paparazzi have known Felina Lopez?

ON THE WAY BACK to the hotel, I reviewed what Sloan had told me. When you hear the phrase "You have to believe me," it's best to keep an eye on your rear end, because you're about to get hosed. Still, the Felina biography was good background, and Leo Lazarnick was a nice lead. Sloan Baker had served her purpose.

Walking into the lobby of the Beverly Hillshire, I almost collided with three plastic surgery disasters coming out of the restaurant. Their faces had been stretched tighter than Saran wrap. With their identical cotton-candy helmets and identical noses, the old gals looked like a pack of interchangeable Mrs. Potato Heads. And, like Mrs. Potato Head, they derived whatever identity they had from their husbands.

There were three messages on the machine. Somebody had been in to clean the room and leave me a Limoges plate with two perfect chocolates in the center. I munched one, trying to get used to this luxury. It was no use; I'd lived too long as a pauper to feel at home in a hotel that looked like a movie set.

I stretched out on the bed, popping the other chocolate in my mouth, and pushed the playback button on the phone.

"Kieran O'Connor? Vernon Ash." He didn't sound like a drug dealer. More like a real-estate agent, or one of those motivational speakers on late-night TV. "I got your message. I'd love to talk to you. We could do a phoner if you want, but I'd rather get together in person. There's something I want to talk to you about myself. How about . . . let's see . . ." I heard pages rustling. "You want to have dinner at Bar Sinister tomorrow night? Say nine-thirty? Give me a call."

Interesting. He sounded more eager to get together than I was. The second message clicked in.

"Hi, 's me." Claudia sounded exhausted. "You got a message yesterday from Jeff Brenner to call him. The mail's just been magazines and bills. Hope everything's okay. I'm whipped. Call me sometime. See ya."

Beep.

"My name is Betty Mann."

I sat up.

"I'm not giving any interviews, but I'd like to talk to you. And I don't want to go through my publicist, so jot this number down." She sounded as tired as Claudia. "That's the phone in my trailer. Set up a time with my assistant, Lesley."

A *click* and then a canned voice told me I had no more messages. Well, dang. I'd gone from pariah to Mr. Popular all of a sudden.

What could Vernon Ash want to talk about? And Betty Bradford Mann—why would she even consent to an interview, even if it was off the record? And which one should I call back first?

I thought about it a minute and dialed Jeff Brenner.

"Well, it beats your old place in Venice," Brenner said, looking around the lobby.

"Let's get out of here. It makes me feel like one of the Beverly Hillbillies. The Beverly Hillshirebilly."

We walked down to Charleville, where Jeff unlocked the passenger door of a new black Lexus. "What happened to the Sentra?" I asked.

"Traded it in." He looked embarrassed. "Tell me the truth. Is it too Hollywood?"

"Depends. Do you have your name painted on your parking space?"

"No. It just says 'Writers.' "

"Then it's fine."

The Lexus had a CD player, which I toyed with as we headed down Wilshire. "So you want to get dinner, or what? I'm in the mood for La Fonda."

"Karen will be home. I thought we'd cook in," he said casually.

When was the last time Claudia and I had cooked in? I couldn't remember. I liked Karen, but sometimes it seemed like she was domesticating Brenner to a frightening degree. The two of us hadn't been out for a meal since he and Karen had tied the knot.

Like me, Brenner had been a freelance writer, but his career had soared as mine had soured. Brenner had moved to New York a while back to become an editor at *Aspect*, "the active magazine for today's active man." In March, right after he and Karen had gotten engaged, a sitcom producer offered Jeff a job as a staff writer, and Jeff moved back to L.A. One month later, *Aspect* folded. Once again, Brenner had landed butter-side-up. It was tempting to think of his life as a series of lucky breaks, but he had set goals and worked toward them with a natural skill and perseverance that completely eluded me. He was one of those people I would have hated if he wasn't my best friend.

We took Wilshire to Ocean and made a right, driving along the bluffs. The sunset sky over the Santa Monica Bay was orange and nail-polish red. I rolled down the window and breathed deeply. Cool salt air, crisp as a potato chip. I was starting to feel the burn from missing a night of sleep.

I rubbed my eyes and asked, "How *is* Karen?"

"Great. We thought we'd barbecue tonight. She's stopping at Pavilions to get some shark steaks."

"Macaroni and cheese would have been fine. 'Course, you people probably don't even remember what that is."

"Yeah, it's caviar for breakfast, caviar for lunch, caviar for dinner."

We stopped at the California incline, which was gridlocked with cars headed home from work and the beach. An ancient van with boogie boards on the top was stalled in the intersection, steam shooting out of its radiator like a teakettle.

"How's Claudia doing on the coffeehouse?"

"Fine. I guess. We don't see each other much."

"You two getting along okay?"

I stared out the windshield. "Somebody better get a fire extinguisher for that van."

Jeff, who knew I was an invertebrate in matters Claudia, dropped the subject.

We drove down the incline and picked up the Pacific Coast Highway, traveling parallel to the ocean, with million-dollar beach cottages on our left and the scrubby brown crags of the Palisades on our right.

"So how is it writing jokes for Becky Burke?"

"Becky's okay. She's just a stand-up comic without any personality. Nothing. She's a tabula rasa with a bad nose job."

"I'll trade you paychecks."

"It's not that much, Kieran. Really. Especially after taxes. Besides, if they're putting you up at the Beverly Hillshire, things can't be too bad."

I hadn't told Jeff about the phone call yet. "Well, then, I'll trade you cars. How's your new place?"

It was his turn to be monosyllabic. "It's okay."

We left the highway at Chautauqua and drove into the Santa Monica Canyon, a woody little enclave of cottages and twisting streets. Two more turns, and we pulled up in front of a Spanish-tiled bungalow with a bay window and a weeping willow in the miniature front yard.

I got out. We were less than a quarter of a mile from the highway, and yet we could have been in the mountains. The street was absolutely silent except for birdsong and the sound of a creek somewhere nearby.

"It doesn't have the charm of my old place in Venice," I said. "Crickets instead of crack dealers. But it's okay."

He cuffed me with my duffel. "You're a smartass, O'Connor."

Karen was at the kitchen island, mixing a salad of bitter greens. She turned around and gave me the smile that all of Los Angeles knew from TV.

Around L.A., Karen Trujillo was a celebrity of sorts. She was a seismologist at Cal Tech, but everyone knew her as the Earthquake Lady. Whenever we had a jolt, Karen would drive out to Pasadena to read the jiggles on the graph, go on camera, and reassure the populace that Palm Springs wasn't about to become beachfront property.

"Hey, Kieran," she said. "We haven't seen you in weeks."

I'm not the one who got married, was my first thought, but I squelched it. "So what went on under the earth's crust today?"

"A couple of little tremors," Karen said. "Nothing anyone could feel, but they were on the Wilshire Fault, so we're watching it."

"The Wilshire? Yikes." We Angelenos are on a first-name basis with our fault lines, the way Floridians are with hurricanes.

"The Wilshire," she said cheerfully. "We're all doomed. Honey, where'd you put the olives?"

We had dinner on a redwood table in the backyard, which was ringed with rosebushes and a stand of evergreens. I ate two pieces of mesquite-grilled shark and half the salad. After dessert, Karen disappeared into the bedroom with a stack of seismology journals while Jeff and I took the rest of the wine down to the creek.

"Brenner, you've done it again."

"What are you talking about?"

"Seriously. Ever since I've known you, it's been like this. The magazine gig. Writing for *Becky*. This house, that car. Hell, even *Jeopardy!*"

Five years ago, we both pitched story ideas about becoming

Jeopardy! contestants—me to the paper and him to a London magazine. I passed the test and never got called back. Jeff made it on the show, where he won a yogurt maker, a case of floor wax, and $47,000 after taxes.

"What's got you so down? This book could be your big break."

"It's not a book. It's a tabloid article in hardcover. It's . . . journalistic necrophilia."

"So it gives you leverage on your next project."

"Sure. Bigger celebrity deaths, juicier scandals. Come on. Don't yank my frank."

"It's not a criminal enterprise, Kieran."

"I know. But I always had contempt for tabloid writers. Now I'm one of them." I stared out at the creek. It was only a small rivulet, clogged with pine needles and dead leaves, but the hills had been denuded in last year's fires. One good storm and Jeff and Karen would have whitewater foaming at the property line. In L.A., you never knew what fresh disaster was just around the corner.

"Brenner—they're not putting me up at the Hillshire because they like me. They put me there because they think it's safe."

I told him about my trip to Mexico, about Felina's murder, everything, ending with the phone call at the Wind & Sea. He whistled.

"Kieran, you don't really think this murder could be related to the book?"

"No. That's just the way they're playing it on TV. You'd have to see this town where she lived. Two separate societies, right on top of each other. Like building Beverly Hills on top of a homeless village. I'm surprised they don't have break-ins all the time; I'm surprised they don't have riots. But that raised another question."

"What?"

"I was under the impression that Felina was writing this book because she needed money. But that house was as nice as this one. Bigger, too. What's that about?"

"Did she own it or was she renting?"

"I don't know."

"Well, what if she got some relocation money from the D.A. or the feds? She could have bought the house back then and just run out of cash."

"I hadn't thought of that." There were a lot of old-money families in Hancock Park and San Marino who had run through their inheritances. From the outside, their houses looked like something out of *Architectural Digest*, but what no one ever saw was the people sitting in unheated rooms, eating Top Ramen. In Southern California, facades are all. "It wouldn't hurt to do a title search, I guess. But none of this explains the call I got, or . . ." I chunked a rock at a pine tree. It landed in a blanket of needles. "Ehh. Enough about this project."

"Okay. Let's talk about you and Claudia."

"Huh?"

"You've been moping around all night, the same way you always do when the two of you are having a fight."

"We're not fighting, Jeff. We're just . . . I don't know." I poured the rest of the wine into my glass. "I just don't know."

"Kieran . . . what *do* you want out of a relationship?"

"*This*," I said. "I want this. A nice house. A backyard. A girlfriend who can manage to keep up a career and a relationship. Shark steaks and friends over for dinner." I killed the chardonnay. "Wineglasses from a crystal shop, not a gas station. Jeez, Brenner. You move through life like Fred Astaire."

He laughed. "Kieran, it's not that easy."

"It wasn't that easy for Fred Astaire either. That's the point." I stood up and brushed damp earth from the seat of my jeans. "He just made it *look* easy."

People think of glamour when they think of the Sunset Strip, but to me it's all about surfaces. Hard surfaces, shiny surfaces. Hot red taillights and the slick sheen of neon and limo glass. That, and death—Sunset is a sinuous avenue where cars skid off embankments in a flash of glass and chrome, where rock stars and runaways OD, where each new generation reinvents the sex/drugs/rock-and-roll lifestyle. The whole passé enchilada that seems so seductive when you're seventeen and invincible.

I stopped at a light. The billboards grew tall and strong on both sides of the street. New ones pimping the latest sound, the latest movie, the latest craze. Old ones, shredded into tatters by the Santa Ana winds. Another twist, another turn, and the music clubs appeared. House of Blues, a zillion-dollar recreation of a Mississippi roadhouse, complete with valet parking and gift shop. The Viper Room. Whisky à Go Go. The Rainbow. The Roxy. And, just before the Strip petered out into Beverly Hills, Bar Sinister—a low-slung black building with no sign. Outside was a line of the usual Sunset suspects: fashion models, guys in Eurotrash suits, and a few haute-couture punks with hundred-dollar spiked haircuts.

I found a semi-legal parking space a few blocks away and walked back. Would-be rock stars were posing on the hoods of cars, air-drumming. Clumps of bored teenagers leaned against buildings, trying to look cool. I smelled clove cigarettes and pot smoke.

The trendoids on the sidewalk glared at me when I walked up to the entrance. When the bouncer found my name on the list and unclipped the velvet rope, they hissed like a pack of geese.

Bar Sinister had been around since the Sixties. The Seeds, the Doors, the Germs, and X had all played there. In the Eighties, it had gone out of business, but recently some Saudi investors had sunk some serious cash into the joint. Now the place was a round space with banquettes and Art Nouveau accents on the walls, like some Forties RKO movie nightclub, down to the old-fashioned candlestick phones on the tables and cigarette girls circling the room. Rumor had it that Bar Sinister was the place to score. If it was uncut and expensive, you could buy it there. I wondered just how reformed a drug dealer Vernon Ash was.

Ash wasn't hard to find. He not only sounded like one of those motivational-speaker slickies from late-night TV, he looked like one, too. A set of large, whiter-than-white teeth was set off by a pink polo shirt and a cream-colored Panama. His skin was tanning-bed bronze. Not a bad-looking package, except for a certain ferret look around his eyes.

I slid into the banquette and we made all the right nice-to-meet-you noises. "Thanks for meeting with me. Really," he said, covering my hand with his. "Tell me about it."

"About what?" Up close, the ferretness was unmistakable. A handsome blond weasel.

"About Felina. All I heard was what I read in the papers. What happened down there?"

I rehashed Via del Paraiso, the beach house, the fax from the Ensenada police. Ash's head was tilted to one side. This was a man who was used to gathering information, assimilating, assessing, processing. Some trendoids walked past the table and gave Ash cool hellos—a tilt of the head, a flick of the palm—but he managed to acknowledge them without breaking focus.

"So it was just a break-in. Nothing to do with the book after all," he concluded.

"Seems that way."

"It sure got you a lot of attention. A publicist couldn't have done a better job. I wish you lots of luck with it, Kieran, I really do."

"Thanks," I said, a little uneasily. Was he really thinking of Felina's death as some kind of cosmic publicity stunt?

"Do the cops have any leads?"

"I don't know. I don't really have any sources on the other side of the border."

"Well, I hope they catch the son of a bitch. Felina was a good person." He caught me looking at him cockeyed. "Hey, I liked Felina. I did, hand to God."

Ash was about to add something, but just then a passerby yelled, "Darling!" and swooped down to smack him on the cheek. "Vern! It's great to have you back! Just the other day I was talking about you to Dylan! You remember Dylan—"

"Good to see you again, Dianne," Ash said, sincere as a politician.

Everything about Dianne was big: big dyed blond hair, big collagen lips, big cartoony, balloony implants that looked about as soft and appealing as granite. Her glance flicked over at me for a moment, and I was about to introduce myself until I realized she was looking over my shoulder. At Bar Sinister, I was just a member of Ash's ever-changing entourage.

"So Dylan and I have started a networking group on Wednesdays at Couchon. The Big Schmooze. Thirty dollars, you get a glass of wine and a chance to meet some really interesting people. Some yutzes, I keep most of 'em out, we have a good time. Can we count on you?"

"Sure."

"Fabulous. Wednesday, Couchon, seven-pee. Love you, mean it." Dianne trundled away, almost mowing down a waitress/waif who was approaching our table like a sleepwalker. She had a gray complexion and ribs that protruded through her blouse. Anorectic junkie waitresses. What an appetizing concept.

Ash got freshwater mozzarella, shiitake ravioli with basil aioli, and a slab of grilled ahi. I ordered a salad, no sprouts, and some tricked-out pasta thing with portobellos.

"You know a lot of people," I said mildly, when the waitress had left.

"Yeah. I can't believe it."

"What?"

"I thought when I got out of jail that people would keep their distance. It's been the opposite, if anything. Guys giving me high fives. Women giving me their phone numbers."

"Richard Ramirez and Ted Bundy had groupies, too."

"Good one. Hey, you're funny."

I shrugged.

Ash checked his watch. "I've got to make a quick call. Can you hold down the fort?" And he was gone behind a thatch of topiary palms, stopping to slap hands at a table of basketball players.

Ash and the food arrived back at the same time, twenty minutes later. There was a hairball of sprouts on my salad.

"She helped send you to jail," I said, picking off the sprouts.

"Hm?"

"Felina."

"Ahh, it wasn't her fault. I never held it against her. Some shitheel from the D.A.'s office got hold of Felina and told her that unless she testified against me she'd be going away, too." He balanced basil leaves and a chunk of mozzarella on his fork. "Felina didn't have enough money to hire a decent lawyer— what's she supposed to do? She shouldn't have to pay for my sins."

"She was pretty vituperative on the stand."

"Vi— What?" A whiter-than-white flash of teeth. "I should hang around you more. Build up my vocabulary."

"Vituperative. Bitter, accusatory. I pulled the old clips. All the D.A. wanted to hear was the drug stuff. She ended up doing a full-on character assassination."

He shrugged, dunked a moon of mozzarella into a pool of

olive oil. "She was just a kid. She hadn't even been out of East L.A. until she was fifteen. Went to Knott's Berry Farm for her *quincinera*. Really, I don't blame her."

"How does someone with a background like that end up as a Hollywood hooker?"

"Those are the only kind that end up being hookers. Young, naive. Her dad was an immigrant. He'd been raising her alone. Hey, these ravioli are fantastic. *Mange.*" He slid a piece onto my plate. "So your deadline's in another month?"

"More or less."

"You got another project firmed up yet?"

"Not exactly."

"Good. I've got a business proposition for you." He flashed that motivational-speaker grin at me again. "How'd you like to write a best-seller?"

"What best-seller?"

Ash passed me a thin folder. "Take a look at this. It's all in there, man. I name names and places. Felina. Dick Mann and a bunch of other people. All it needs is a ghostwriter."

I opened it to the title page. *Shooting Stars: My Life as a Celebrity Drug Dealer.*

"Well," I said. "Well."

"I started it in prison, man. It's all in there. Names and places. Dick Mann and everybody else you could imagine. But I'm not a writer. So whaddaya think?" He beamed. "Let's be real. Nobody gives two shits about Felina's book. What I'm offering here is a chance to get your name on a real best-seller. I'm gonna start the bidding at a hundred K. Get the suckers and the chumps out of the way at the start."

"You've had offers?"

"I don't even have an agent, man. This is ground-floor. Whaddaya say?"

"I'd say . . . that's interesting. Can I take this and look it over?"

"Sure. Hey, I value your opinion. And that's my beeper number on the front. Twenty-four seven, you got me? Hey, you like shiitake? Take these, I'm not hungry. I've gotta go make another call."

There was a flyer for a band called Phlegm Banquet stuck under my wiper, and a fuschia-lipsticked kiss on my side-view mirror. Even money on whether the kiss was from a guy or a girl.

I made a right on Doheny Boulevard, heading off the Strip and back toward the Beverly Hillshire. Even at one A.M., Doheny was a parking lot. Sitting in the traffic snarl, I felt like I needed a flea dip.

It wasn't just Vernon Ash, or Bar Sinister, or the lousy trendy food, or Dianne the schmooze queen. It was everything. Mostly, though, it was Ash's book proposal, which was sitting on the passenger seat next to me.

Looking at it, I'd had the same queasy vertigo I felt sitting in Jack Danziger's office. It didn't matter what you did anymore. Sell your body. Sell drugs. Have a drug problem, or anorexia, or beriberi. Be the father of a mass murderer, or knock off a couple of people yourself. Everyone's got a book these days.

And I could remember when everyone in Hollywood wanted to direct.

How dumb could you get? True, Hollywood drug dealers aren't exactly MENSA candidates, but what could Vernon Ash have been thinking when he handed over his book proposal to a writer who was compiling another book on the same subject? "Theft of intellectual property" was the official term, but there was nothing intellectual about Vernon Ash.

Hadn't it occurred to Ash that I might rip him off? Dope dealers may not be smart, but they're paranoids, always on alert for a potential rip-off. The more I thought about it, the more it smelled fishy, from his eagerness to meet me up to the moment when he handed me his life story.

There was something in there that he wanted me to know. Or, more likely, something he wanted me to believe.

Down the hill, at the Santa Monica–Doheny intersection, two cars had collided in a spray of broken glass and chrome. A headlight dangled from the bumper of one car like an eye popped from its socket. Traffic was completely stopped, and a few drivers were leaning on their horns. To hell with it. I nosed my car into the far lane and hooked a right onto Elevado, crossing the border into Beverly Hills. It was the wrong way back to the hotel, but I couldn't stand the traffic.

All of BH is rare air, but some air is rarer than others. The "flats" (south of Sunset) are preferable to the "hills" above Sunset, and "south-of-Wilshire" is declassé compared to north of the Boulevard. This was the flats, north of Wilshire, and it was posh.

At this time of night, the Beverly Hills flats were like a closed museum of Tudors and ranch-styles and Norman castles with hot tubs under the turrets. Every single house had a private security sign stuck in the front lawn, even though the police station was only a few blocks away. Security companies made a fortune installing cut-proof phone lines and luxury bedrooms with foot-thick concrete walls. Some of the most paranoid ultra-rich were even installing microchips under their children's skin to foil potential kidnappers. At Elm, I caught a glimpse of the Menendez house, which had enjoyed a brief vogue as a photo-op for tourists who got tired of the Chinese Theater.

No one was on the streets, and the only other car I saw was a slow-cruising sedan from one of the ubiquitous private security patrols. It had a leather "car bra" on the front. In L.A., you see more bras on the cars than you do on the women.

Sometimes things happen for a reason. If it wasn't for the BHPD cruiser parked on the next block, I wouldn't have slowed down when I got to Foothill, and if I hadn't slowed down when I got to Foothill, I wouldn't have had a flicker of déjà vu.

Betty Bradford Mann lived on Foothill.

I had been at Mann's house several years ago. It was a kick-off party for a charity event: Rich people were going to play tennis or golf in Hawaii or Mexico, and somehow this was going to raise money for kids with CF or CP or something. All I remembered about Mann's place was an enormous leaded-glass window on the second floor, brilliant as a chandelier.

It took two trips up and down the block before I found the place. Since I'd been there, someone—Dick? Betty?—had enclosed the place with a wall and a privet hedge. It had a newish look, and I wondered if the extra security had been added since Dick's death. I eased the car up to the curb but didn't shut off the engine.

A speaker grille was concealed in a fake rock where the driveway bisected the sidewalk. Behind the barricade was a rambling two-story faced with gray stone and clapboards, and the top-floor window that was my landmark. Tonight it was as dark as the rest of the houses on the street. Not a branch moved in the yard.

As I watched, the glass lit up.

Someone was standing there, a dark smudge behind brilliant prisms.

Watching me.

I put the Buick in gear and drove away, and saw the light extinguish in my rearview as I reached the corner.

TWO

= 7 =

THE ADDRESS TOOK ME up into the low foothills that separated Hollywood from the San Fernando Valley, just east of Griffith Park. Beaters and hoopties lined the street, their wheels dug into the hard dirt at the side of the road. Smog-burnt palm trees stuck into the sky like spent matches. Mexican kids played kickball in the street. They drew back grudgingly as my car approached.

I found Rascon Circle and pulled over in front of a scumbly little cottage that looked as if it should have a junk sale planted permanently in the front yard. More dusty palm trees lurched over the house. The only thing new was a gleaming onyx van that sat in the driveway. It had silvery antennas on top and windows tinted an illegal shade of jet black.

Dead grass crunched under my feet, and the doorbell gave off a clunking sound instead of a chime. I waited.

"Hey, come take a look at my new toy."

I turned around and saw the head of an enormously fat man sticking out of the van window. It looked like a Halloween pumpkin gone mushy.

"Leo Lazarnick?"

" 'S me. Come take a look at my new baby."

I poked my head inside. It reeked of new car and some chemical that I'd smelled in the photo lab down at the paper.

Lazarnick was sitting behind the wheel, in a bucket seat that appeared custom-made for his incredible girth. Behind him was a tricked-out cockpit of a dashboard; I recognized a telephone, a fax, a police scanner, a radar detector, and a CB radio, but there were half a dozen other devices that I could only guess at.

"I can live in this motherfucker for a week if I have to." Lazarnick picked some flexible metal signs off the seat next to him. "Here, take a load off."

I sat in the passenger seat next to him and smelled something else: sweat and Gold Bond Medicated Powder. He probably rubbed it between his legs to prevent chafing. The metal signs were magnetized, the kind contractors stick on the doors of their vans: Alameda Home Security, Electryx Enterprises, Inc., California Cable, Echo Park Lock & Key.

"Unmarked black van parked on the street, somebody's gonna notice, right? I just slap one of those bad boys on the door and I'm invisible."

Invisible; right. It would take more than a fake sign to make Leo Lazarnick disappear. It wasn't just his morbid obesity; his fat was so pale and suety, he looked like he was melting. A gelatinous roll of fat oozed over the back of his shirt collar like a goiter. And then there was the sweaty cornstarch smell, which was already overwhelming the scent of new car, making my lunch rumble.

It was hard to imagine Felina Lopez—no matter how young or innocent—even touching this man.

I looked around the rest of the van. It contained a refrigerator, a microwave, and a three-basin steel sink with jugs of chemicals under it. A small light table was folded up against the facing wall. Tucked next to the fridge was a stack of those heavy paper funnels that truckers use on long hauls.

Flash.

I turned around. Lazarnick was holding a Nikon. *Flash.* This time it caught me directly in the eyes, blinding me.

"Knock it off." I hate having my picture taken as much as I hate being interviewed. Most reporters do.

"Hey, you want something, you gotta give something back, huh? Lemme get a couple in color." *Flash. Flash. Flash.*

His hands looked like piles of mashed potatoes, but his fingers were surprisingly dexterous little trotters. When he was done, he popped out the film and put it in one of the many pockets on his chinos. "Come on in the house."

"What the hell do you want pictures of me for?"

He climbed out of the van with some effort. "Hey, you never know. You could win a Pulitzer. Or you could get shot on the freeway. Either way, I could find somebody to buy it."

Something beeped. He pulled a cell phone out of his pocket and flipped it open. "Brad? Yeah, sure. Lemme get in the house. Where's it going? On the cover? Two thousand and don't argue." He balanced the tiny phone under his chins while he unlocked the front door. I followed him inside. "Come on, Brad, don't try to screw the pooch. Two K and it's yours. . . . Yeah, yours as in yours. Publish it every week for all I care."

The Nazi Paparazzi might have blown a wad on his van, but he sure hadn't spent any money on his house. The hall was dank, with faded wallpaper and more smells: dirty sneakers, fried food, ripe cat box. An old roseglass chandelier held a single bulb. Putty-colored file cabinets lined the walls.

It was what *wasn't* there that got my attention. The photographers I knew at the paper had framed and matted copies of their work displayed proudly all over their homes: fire shots, riot shots, the Lakers in action. But in the long hall that ran through Leo Lazarnick's house, the walls were bare of everything but seeping water stains.

"Come on, Braddy, come on. . . . Nah, you can't see the nipple, but you can see everything but."

I followed Lazarnick into a kitchen that looked like my old apartment after the earthquake. Lazarnick yanked open the door on a vintage icebox and pulled out a bottle of Mountain Dew. "Okay, okay. With that kind of budget, you can't expect much. Lemme see what else I got on her."

He clumped out of the kitchen, leaving me alone to eyeball the place.

Cases of Mountain Dew were stacked under the table. A mousetrap sat baited with peanut butter. The litter box in the corner was filled with a couple weeks' worth of kitty nuggets, which explained at least one of the smells. A battered kitchen table was hidden under strata of photographs, contact sheets, and magazines that had been folded back and marked with grease pencil. The credits read LEO LAZARNICK PHOTOGRAPHY.

Under an old pizza box was another stack of glossies, some with orange grease-pencil crop marks. I flipped through a few pictures. Long shots taken at movie premieres, mostly. I found a shot of Princess Diana climbing out of a limousine, which was vaguely disquieting, and a hospital shot of Elizabeth Taylor with a hose in her nose. More premiere shots, these grainier, as if taken a long way off at night. A topless shot of a young TV star in bed. She looked more drugged than asleep.

And a photo of Betty Bradford Mann.

It was a long shot, taken from at least several hundred yards away, probably snapped from a helicopter or a hillside. The actress was coming down a short flight of stairs in a plain business suit, her eyes hidden by Jackie O dark glasses. An arm came into the left side of the frame, supporting her. She was holding the hand of a sober-faced, almost painfully thin little boy with dark hair. In her other hand was a single rose.

The Nazi Paparazzi had crashed Dick Mann's funeral.

"*Fuckwad!*"

Lazarnick was standing a foot behind me. I almost peed my pants. For such a behemoth, he could move on cat's paws when he wanted to.

"Fuckwad! He wants to use it on the cover and he offers me four hundred bucks? Fuck him. Fuck him to hell!" His face was the color of an eggplant; a prolapsed vein on his temple was vibrating. "I'll sell it to *Celeb* for a dollar before Brad gets it now! I'll fucking walk in and set it on fucking fire on his fucking desk!"

With a normal person, I might have been ready to call the EMS. Obviously Leo Lazarnick had these grand mal tantrums about twenty times a day.

". . . and when that fucking fairy has to report to those guineas he works for and tell them that he lost out just 'cause he was trying to Jew me down a few bucks—"

Next to the Kurds, I couldn't think of a minority he'd missed insulting.

He noticed the photo in my hand, and the squall subsided

as quickly as it had come. "You like that? It's got a great story behind it."

"This was taken at Dick Mann's funeral?"

He nodded. "See, they were gonna bury Mann out in Simi Valley for some reason—this half-assed little cemetery off the freeway. And the tabs were making noises about big bucks for the best photo of the wife. Now, Forest Lawn, Westwood, the *real* boneyards, I know 'em like the back of my hand, I can *work* with those places. This joint, they closed it down for the morning so no one could get in. Harry Carbo, that fuckwad, he hired a helicopter to fly over so he could hang off the bottom and get the shot. Well, I can't fit my fat ass onto no chopper, so I had to think. Know what I did?"

I shook my head.

"There was this freeway down the road."

"You shot it from the overpass."

His neck rolls bulged with pride. "Nah. I went up there beforehand, but the angle was just *that* much off. So I shot it from *under* the overpass. Climbed up there, right where the concrete meets the dirt. Turns out up under the rebar lives some wetback. Well, I told him he was gonna be my assistant for the day. Still didn't know if it was gonna work, but with these lenses I got from the government, I thought it would work. Carbo, he's dangling off his chopper, makin' a fool of himself, and I send the wetback out on his belly like a snake. I'm hanging on to my wetback amigo's feet, yelling at him to press the button and hold it steady, or I swear I'll let go his feet and drop his ass right into the middle of the 118 freeway. He shot off a couple rolls, I gave him twenty bucks for his help, drove the film over to *Celeb,* and picked up a check for twelve thou."

"Wow," I said, for lack of anything better.

Lazarnick went over to the fridge and popped another Dew. "You're writing a book about Felina, huh?"

"I was writing it *with* Felina. Before she died."

"Whereja get my name? Those assholes at *Headline Journal?*" He didn't wait for an answer. "More fuckwads. I gave them first rights of refusal. First rights and a damned fair price."

"First rights to what?"

"The nude shots, dumbshit. What else?"

Nude shots?

"I didn't hear back from 'em for almost twenty-four hours. They dicked me around so long that I finally passed. I knew there'd be other offers. Like you." He grinned. "And if you don't want 'em, I got plenty of sources. I'll sell 'em in England if I have to."

"How long have you had these nude shots of Felina?"

"Fifteen, twenty years."

"How'd you get them?" I tried to keep my voice casual.

He took a gulp of Dew. "I was freelancing, shooting concerts at the Whisky and the Troubadour. I met up with this guy who ran a couple of titty rags."

"Like *Playhouse* and *Hustler?*"

"Nah. These were newsprint. Like *Screw*. He sold 'em in vending machines on Hollywood Boulevard. Anyway, he told me I could pick up some money doing girlie shots. There were a million of 'em just like Felina who hung around the clubs, hoping to score with a musician or whatever. And they all needed money."

I pulled out my tape recorder. "Mind if I turn this on?"

"Put it away. I'm not giving you any interview."

"Come on, Leo—"

"Hey, don't try to screw the pooch. I thought you were here to buy some pictures. You're not interested, there's the door."

"Can I see the pictures?"

He grinned. "Maybe."

"Why didn't you sell them during the Vernon Ash trial?"

"Couldn't get enough money."

"Isn't some money better than none?"

"Hey, it was a gamble. But I'm a good gambler." Green soda pop dribbled down his chins like antifreeze. "And now Jack Danziger's gonna be the payoff. You tell him that I'll give him a good deal, but that they ain't gonna be cheap. And tell him not to dick me around. Remember, I don't need the money, so if you're not serious, *adios*."

I followed him back down the dingy hallway to the back of the house. Lazarnick led me past a darkroom with a red light-bulb over the doorjamb and stopped in front of a door locked with a double dead bolt. He took a key ring out of his pocket.

The room was so bright I blinked. White walls and over-head fluorescent fixtures made it feel like a laboratory, or an operating theater. All around the perimeter of the room were more file cabinets, each with laser-printed labels stuck neatly to the fronts of the drawers. Two light tables were covered with contact sheets and eyepieces. A paper shredder was balanced on a forty-gallon trash drum filled with confetti, next to a fax machine. There weren't any personal items anywhere. If Leo Lazarnick had an inner life, I still hadn't seen it. Leo Lazarnick was a picture-taking machine, the way a shark was an eating machine.

"Welcome to the Starship Enterprise," he said.

I walked around, looking at the file cabinets. One of them—a big one—was labeled NUDES.

"You still do nude shots, Leo?"

"Hell, no. There's no money in that anymore, unless it's someone famous. Video and the Internet killed that market. But I've still got all my originals. I keep everything. Ev-ree-thing."

"Why?"

"Jesus, you are stupid, aren't you?" He sighed. "One day some dumbass shot a picture of O.J. Simpson. Turned out that the Juice was wearing a certain pair of shoes, and bam! Welcome to a new tax bracket."

He used the key ring on a file cabinet drawer labeled NUDES: K–M, selected a manila envelope—so old its edges were foxed and furred—and took out a stack of black-and-whites.

"Where'd you take these?"

"Christ, I dunno. Probably the backyard of my old place on Bronson." Lazarnick's fat thumb riffled through the stack, making a quick count.

His cell phone went off again. He handed me the stack of photos. "Bet that's Brad changed his mind. Here, take a look. Braddy? Thought that was you. . . ."

I flipped through the stack of five-by-sevens.

It was Felina, all right. Black and white and topless to boot. The face looked about sixteen; the body, twenty-five. There were no dates on the back, but from the hairstyles and the few clothes she had on, I guessed they were fifteen to twenty years old. Some were indoors, some were taken under a tree, but Felina wasn't wearing a blouse in any of them. The focus wasn't sharp and the lighting was downright terrible, but the guys who thumbed quarters into the nudie racks on Hollywood Boulevard weren't looking for beaver shots of Ansel Adams quality.

The "money shot" was the last one. Felina, reclining in a chaise longue. She was totally nude, legs spread. Her hair was a-tousle and her tongue poked out of her mouth awkwardly.

I tried to figure out what was so profoundly disturbing about it. It wasn't the breasts or the spread legs. It was the very amateureness: the sight of a teenage girl forced into a ridiculous parody of a centerfold. Not yet twenty, and already a commodity. She hadn't mastered the cheesecake tease yet.

It felt like a mug shot.

This was interesting stuff, but ultimately meaningless. If Lazarnick wouldn't give me an interview, there was virtually nothing I could use for the book, except for a paragraph or two about her days at the Sunset Strip rock clubs.

I shoved the glossies back in their envelope. They went halfway in and then caught on something: a piece of paper.

"Well, if you don't want it after all, why the fuck are you bothering me, Brad? Tell that boss of yours this little dick-around is gonna cost him next time I get something he really wants. . . ."

Lazarnick's fax beeped, and a piece of paper began sliding out. He walked over to the fax, mumbling into the phone the whole way.

I pulled out what was in the envelope.

It was an old photocopy that had faded to a dingy gray. At the top was typed the words MODEL RELEASE. Below was some boilerplate releasing all rights, present and future, to Leonard H. Lazarnick.

At the bottom was a signature: Eduardo Lopez.

Eduardo?

Lazarnick was scanning his fax, yelling into the phone. "That's it! I'm telling you for the last time. Take it or leave it."

I took it.

ON THE WAY BACK to the hotel, I stopped at Kiri-Dog for lunch. I could have ordered Chateaubriand from room service and charged it to Jack Danziger, but a burrito sounded better. My palate was no more sophisticated than the rest of me. Besides, I needed to think, and I wanted comfort food.

Kiri-Dog was a weatherbeaten lunch stand on a nasty stretch of Santa Monica Boulevard. The clientele was mostly teenage hustlers and runaways, but I was addicted to their Kosher Burrito: hot dogs, scrambled eggs, and pastrami thrown together in a tortilla and glued together with neon-orange grease. God only knew where the name Kosher Burrito came from—it was about as rabbinically approved as bacon with ranch dressing—but I'd been addicted to it for years.

I got a Kosher Deluxe and an order of O-rings, sat down at a picnic table overlooking a car wash and a film-developing lab, and pulled the piece of paper out of my pocket.

There it was, in clear, unmistakable cursive: Eduardo Lopez. Felina's father?

It was possible. After all, the Felina in Lazarnick's photos could have been only sixteen or seventeen. The body was centerfold material, but the face was Pedophile City.

Queasiness set in, and it had nothing to do with the burrito. What kind of father would let his teenage daughter be photographed topless?

At the next table a gaggle of underage throwaways and prostitutes was splitting a single order of fries. One girl squirted plastic packets of ketchup into a cup of water, making tomato soup. She wore a pair of Daisy Dukes and a halter top pulled down to expose bee-bite boobs. I put her at fourteen.

Who was I kidding? This was *Hollywood*. Hell, if a movie role was at stake, some parents would send their daughters over to the casting director's house, wearing a red ribbon and a smile.

Maybe Eduardo Lopez was the worst kind of scum—maybe even a child molester himself. That would explain the nights at the Troubadour, the drugs, the prostitution. Weren't most hookers abused as kids, or was that just an urban myth?

I took another bite of burrito and licked up the grease that ran down my hand. It still didn't fit. Somewhere I had gotten the idea that the Lopezes were Old Country Catholics. I didn't even know if Lopez spoke English.

Perhaps he had signed it without being able to read it. Perhaps Felina hadn't told him the nature of the pictures.

Perhaps she hadn't known what they were going to be herself.

Pulling my old Buick into the porte cochere of the Beverly Hillshire, I could feel my stomach clench. Once I could have put away a Kosher Burrito and an order of rings and be ready for an ice-cream sandwich. Now all I wanted for dessert was Maalox.

I bought a small bottle of the stuff at extortionist hotel

prices and was leaving the gift shop when someone slugged me with a purse.

"You *schmuck!*"

I whirled. This time Sloan's purse caught me in the breadbasket and pitched me into a display of duty-free Fantabulous Fakes Fragrances, knocking vials of "Gorgio" and "Channel No. 5" to the carpet.

"I've been waiting for you for two hours in that goddamn lobby!"

"Sloan," I hissed, "can we discuss this somewhere private? Like my room?"

She stalked out of the gift shop and headed for the elevators. I picked up my Maalox and trotted after her. If she'd had a tail, it would have been switching. She wasn't wearing any makeup, and her hair was pulled back into a ponytail. Without the makeup, her resemblance to Felina was almost nil.

The elevator was empty, thank God. I jabbed a button and a voice announced "Thirty-four" in English, French, and Japanese.

"You mind telling me what this is about?"

Sloan sagged against the back wall of the elevator. "I got a call. On my unlisted home phone."

The elevator went cold for a second.

"What kind of call?" I said slowly.

"Someone who knew I had talked to you."

"Someone threatened you?"

"Yes. No. Not threatened. But he knew about us meeting at the gym. He even knew what I had to drink."

". . . Okay. This is not good. But it's not necessarily something to worry—"

"Easy for you to say! You're not the one getting mysterious phone calls!"

I clammed up until we got to my room.

Sloan helped herself to a five-dollar fruit drink from the mini-bar and plopped down on the sofa.

"Make yourself at home," I said.

"Thanks."

So much for irony. "Tell me about this call."

"I was at home a couple of hours ago, about to take a shower. The phone rings, and this voice goes, 'How was your lunch?' I go, 'What lunch?' and he goes, 'Your lunch at Smooth Moo. You didn't even finish your shake.'

"Well, I go, 'Who is this?' Right then, I reach down and pick up my cat, 'cause I'm scared. And he laughs again and goes, 'Just a friend. By the way, that's a mighty pretty cat you've got there. Pretty little pussycat.' And he hangs up."

"Wait. He could see you?"

"The front drapes were open, just a little bit. But I'm on the third floor. He would've had to have binoculars, or a telescope."

Sloan swigged more guava juice and hugged herself, rocking back and forth gently. The story was far-fetched. A little too elaborate. If it wasn't for the call I had gotten, I wouldn't have believed it. But I had. And I did.

"Sloan . . . I got one of those calls, too. He didn't say anything openly threatening, but it felt pretty menacing anyway. And I couldn't make out the voice either."

"Oh, I *know* who it was," Sloan said. "That's why I'm scared."

"Who?"

"Brooks Levin."

"I— Are you sure?"

She nodded.

"Holy . . ."

"You got that right," she said, and popped another bottle of juice.

Hollywood is a forgiving place. You can cheat on your wife, neglect your children, shoot heroin for twenty years, have an orgy with the Mormon Tabernacle Choir, and still make a comeback—as long as you're willing to share the details in front of God and Oprah. Even by today's standards, though, there are still some forms of trouble—child molestation, multiple murder—that might just kill a career dead-bang.

That's why Brooks Levin was on the auto-dialer of every publicist and agent in town, right next to Police, Fire, and Spago.

Levin referred to himself as a security consultant, but soldier of fortune was more accurate. Drop a dime to Levin and your troubles would go away. Levin assembled teams of publicists, defense lawyers, potential witnesses, whatever it took. He worked for celebrities, defending them against the tabloids, and then turned around and defended the tabloids against celebrity suits. On top of everything, he refused all interviews, which only added to his myth as a shadow kingpin of Hollywood.

Brooks Levin was always on the same side: the side of whoever got there first with the money.

Sloan stared at me with a look somewhere between wonder and dread. "What the fuck are you working on here?"

I looked out the window, down at the shoppers jaywalking

across Rodeo Drive. Somebody didn't want her talking to me. Somebody didn't want this book written. Somebody who was wealthy or powerful enough to hire Brooks Levin.

"I don't know, Sloan," I told her. "I really don't know anymore."

We powwowed for a while, long enough for her to demolish another fruit drink from the minibar along with a can of macadamia nuts. I stuck to my Maalox. It was like drinking a puree of minted chalk, but it did the trick. My stomach was doing flip-flops and it wasn't from the burrito.

"So how did you recognize Levin's voice, anyway?" I asked. "He doesn't do interviews. I've never seen him on TV."

"He'd called me before."

"He'd called you before?" I yelped. "Why?"

She opened up the French doors leading to the terrace and tightened her hands on the railing. I followed her out into the warm summer dusk.

"It was a few weeks ago. When Dick died. My contact at *Celeb* was pressuring me for a story. They were calling two or three times a day, but I wouldn't do it."

"You *did* do it."

"Levin *made* me. I didn't want to tell you that."

"What do you mean?"

"I picked up my unlisted line one morning and this voice said, 'Have you checked your mail?' Then he hung up. I went downstairs to my mailbox, which was locked, by the way. Well, the mail hadn't come, but there *was* a letter there. Addressed to the head of the agency I work for. It had everything I'd ever talked to *Celeb* about. Names and dates."

"A dossier. And that would have gotten you fired from the agency."

She snorted. "At least."

"But how can you be sure it was Brooks Levin on the phone?"

"I didn't know then. But the letter was dated two days ahead. That part was highlighted. I got the message. If I didn't talk to *Celeb*, they would send the letter to the agency. So I called the magazine and they put me on hold for a couple of minutes. When my contact got on the line, I started to yell at him. And then he goes, real casual-like, 'Did Brooks Levin get hold of you yet?'"

"So I talked. And they got their story." She spread her hands helplessly. "They had all the checks they'd written me, endorsed with my signature. What was I supposed to do?" She stared at me. "And what am I supposed to do now? Huh?"

I tried to process it all. Was Levin still working for *Celeb*? Could the tabloid want my book stopped?

But why? *Celeb's* story had already run. They had deep pockets to buy any source they wanted; a network of "friends" who owed them favors; and, of course, Gina Guglielmelli, who made me look like Jimmy Olsen. It wouldn't be *Celeb* Levin was working for now. But who?

"We've got to make a police report," I said.

"No."

"Sloan, this might be dangerous."

"I've been arrested before. I'm not going to deal with the cops."

"Not a regular police report. We can call the LAPD Threat Management Unit."

Los Angeles has the only police force in the world with a special stalking department, which says a lot about the number of celebrities *and* psychos in the city. They keep tabs on several thousand stalkers, and about one-third of their cases, from the gossip I'd heard, were industry-related.

"You can do it alone," said Sloan. "I won't cooperate. And if you do—"

The phone rang. We both started.

"Don't answer it!" yelled Sloan.

"This isn't *Mission: Impossible*. It's not gonna explode." I picked up the receiver.

"Kieran?"

"Claude. Hey." My breath came out in a big whoosh.

"I haven't heard from you. What's going on?"

"Just been busy. I'm sorry." I mouthed the words "my girlfriend" to Sloan. She went into the bathroom.

"Any more problems with the press?"

"No. Everything's quiet. I'm just busy right now. What's news with you?"

"Canem's coming along. We're almost ready." She paused. "Are you still planning on coming to the opening?"

"Of course I am. Why wouldn't I?"

"Don't get irritated. You've already mentioned you were busy twice in thirty seconds."

"Claude, you know I wouldn't miss that."

"Okay, okay. Just checking." Her voice turned suspiciously cheery. "My sister flew in this morning. As a surprise."

"Lydia? Is she still separated from Charlie?"

Sloan was running water. It sounded like she was filling the tub. What the . . .

"Yeah. So she's come down to help me get the coffeehouse ready. Isn't that *nice?* Listen, she wants to say hi."

"No, Claude, please, I'm not up for Lydia—"

"And she's right here! I'll talk to you later."

"Kieran!"

"Lyd. Hi." I dragged the phone over to the bathroom door. Sloan *was* filling the tub.

"Claudia tells me you're busy, so I won't keep you. Listen, I made reservations for you and me and Miss Claudia Marie at The Restaurant for day after tomorrow, eight-thirty. It's on me. Or, rather, it's on the Diners Club card of Charles P. Boudreaux, my perhaps-soon-to-be ex-husband."

"Lydia, I'm really swamped right—"

"There are to be no excuses, Kieran O'Connor. I flew two thousand miles just to see you two. And I'm not coming to L.A. without sampling the culinary genius of Hans-Peter Jungenhoffman. I was reading about him on the Internet, and they say—"

"I gotta go, Lydia. Please."

"Go, go! I'll see you at eight-thirty. Day after tomorrow!" She made a kissy noise and hung up.

I knocked on the bathroom door. "Sloan?"

No answer. The taps shut off.

I pounded. "Sloan? Are you all right?"

Sloan threw the door open. She was wrapped in my complimentary hotel bathrobe and a turban made of a Beverly Hillshire towel.

"Can I have some privacy?"

"What the hell are you doing?"

"Knitting a sweater. What does it look—"

"You can't take a bath in my room!"

She jabbed me in the sternum. "Listen, you got me into this mess. You and your damn interview. I've got to get cleaned up somewhere. I'm scared to death to go back to my own apartment, and it's all your fault."

I started to object, but there wasn't much higher ground for me to take. She sensed my waffling, and that bit of hesitation cost me big-time.

"Thank you," she said primly. *"Now can I please have a little bit of damn privacy?"*

The door slammed. There was a bit of dainty splashing. After a minute, the tubside TV went on.

"Make yourself at home."

"I will," she yelled.

Irony. It's lost on some people.

THE SKY ABOVE THE Hollywood Hills was smudgy with dusk. Last time I'd looked up, it had been mid-afternoon. I saved the file I was working on and stood. My back made noises like someone walking on bubble wrap.

One thing about hiding out from Brooks Levin: I was getting a lot of work done. I had been holed up in the suite for two days, slapping together the first and only draft of *Mann's Woman*, interrupted only by the actor/model/whatever who brought me room service twice a day.

"When do I get to see a few pages of this masterpiece?" asked Jocelyn, during one of her hurry-hurry-nudge-nudge calls.

"Next week."

"Next week is for Jack Danziger. I want to see what you have now. Fed Ex me a copy."

"It's crap."

"It's a quickie bio of a Hollywood hooker, Peaches."

"I know, but I still want it to be good."

"*Good* isn't the point," Jocelyn told me. "*Done* is."

I popped a couple of Aleve—one for the spine, one for the carpal tunnel—and lay down on the sofa to do some back-stretching exercises. The pot of coffee in my stomach sloshed around. I had to pee like Secretariat.

The phone rang. I rolled over to pick it up, hoping it was Lydia calling to cancel our dinner. The opening of Canem was tomorrow night. Wouldn't Claudia have too many last-minute things to do? I didn't know. I hadn't had the motivation—or the nerve—to call her back since Sloan Baker had taken up residence in my bedroom.

"Hi, dear. Just called to give you some rah-rah-sis-boom-bah."

"Hi, Kitty." *Snap*. Something in my back surrendered.

Kitty still didn't know about Brooks Levin. No one did. I had considered talking to Jocelyn, just to have someone to tell, but decided against it, remembering how she had panicked after that first call. Under her agent mask was a vicious maternalism.

"You all set to meet Betty Mann tomorrow?" chirped Kitty.

I had phoned Lesley, Betty Bradford Mann's assistant, who said Betty was shooting a TV movie and didn't have much spare time. We finally agreed I could meet the star in her trailer for a quick lunch.

"She must be having second thoughts. I got a voice mail this morning from her publicist."

"Well, that's understandable. Who is her publicist?"

"Susan D'Andrea."

"Oh," said Kitty. *Oh* was right; Susan didn't let her clients fart without her permission. She looked upon the working press the way a Mormon did NAMBLA.

I heard the metallic *snick* of the card key in the door. Sloan walked in wearing a maillot that rose up in the crotch to reveal what Claudia called a "cameltoe." Her hair was wet.

"Kitty, why do you think Betty would even talk to me?"

"She probably thinks she can disarm you, dear. But you can be pretty disarming yourself."

"Maybe. The whole thing's off the record, anyway. Susan repeated that about eight times."

"Well, call me when you're done and let me know how it went. I've never met her, but everyone says Betty's really a lovely person."

"Thanks. Have a good night."

"Okey-dokey, artichokey," she said, and rang off.

"Who was that?" Sloan ran a triangle of pita through some baba ghanoush and popped it in her mouth.

"Kitty Keyes. And do you mind, Sloan? I was saving that for a snack."

Her response was a march into the bathroom. The Beverly Hillshire maids had already made two towel deliveries today.

"Sloan, can I get in there first? I've got to pee and change clothes. I'm having dinner with my girlfriend and her sister."

The shower went on. I groaned.

Sharing a deluxe suite at a five-star hotel with a Hollywood hooker was a fantasy that most men could only dream about. Unfortunately, the reality was less *Pretty Woman* than it was *Pretty Annoying Woman*.

When Sloan had begged me to stay for "a night or two," I still felt slightly guilty—although not quite guilty enough to let her do it. What finally swayed me was the chance to get some more dirt on Felina. Having a source underfoot seemed like it would have its advantages.

Underfoot, yes. Source, no. Sloan had left the hotel exactly once since she'd arrived two days ago, and that was a jaunt to her apartment to pack a few things. The "few things" were a stack of fake Vuitton suitcases that took two bellboys to bring up to the room. My closet was now crowded with expensive outfits and the bathroom sink looked like Bloomingdale's makeup counter. Worse, since I was working on the book in the living room area, Sloan had commandeered the bedroom, granting me the sofa.

And I still hadn't managed to corner her for an interview.

Sighing, I went out on the balcony. On the chaise were two things: Vernon Ash's manuscript and a copy of the East Los Angeles White Pages.

No matter how bad my Felina book turned out, it would look like *Finnegan's Wake* next to what Ash had set down. Even a literary mercenary like Jack Danziger would have round-filed *Shooting Stars*. It was a series of disconnected, dated reminiscences, written in the run-on monotony of a coke rap. The only real names belonged to dead stars whose drug use was part of the public record. And there wasn't a word about his trial and conviction, much less Felina.

I had assumed that Ash gave me his manuscript because there was something in there he wanted me to know, or believe. What that might be I had no idea. Maybe he *was* just stupid enough to hand off a manuscript to a total stranger. As research material, it was useless.

And the phone book; oh, God. There were more Lopezes in Southern California than there were Smiths. I had begun with the Eduardos and then moved on to the E's. I had found only one or two households where someone spoke English, and those were only the people who didn't hang up the minute they heard a gringo on the line. Apparently an English-speaking voice meant one thing: *la migra, immigración.* There were columns upon columns of other Lopezes, and no guarantee that the mysterious Eduardo was among them, much less still alive.

I was tempted to cancel dinner with Lydia and Claudia, but I needed to get out of the room for a while. To me, writing is like making a mosaic—each word to be polished, fussed over, and laid lovingly into position—but there just wasn't time. I felt like I was painting a fresco with a roller.

After I'd left my copy of the manuscript with the concierge to be copied, I walked over to Canon Drive. The eatery where I was meeting the Dubuisson sisters was called The Restaurant. In Beverly Hills and West L.A., there was one of these trattorie on every block, catering to the locals' inexhaustible taste for herbed olive oil and buffalo mozzarella served up by pretty little Ron Goldmans. Thank God Lydia was treating. Thirty bucks for a plate of nouvelle spaghetti was a little beyond my wallet.

Before I could speak to the maître d', I heard: *"Kieran!"*

Lydia was at a table in the center of the room, waving her napkin. As if I could have missed her. Most heavy women tend to dress conservatively, but Lydia did the opposite. Her dress was white with black polka dots, topped off with a picture hat in a reverse color scheme. You could have set a drink on her shoulderpads. Claudia was nowhere in evidence.

Lydia seized me in a dramatic embrace, then just as quickly held me at arm's length. "Careful of the tits; they're sore as hell. Kieran, you should fall down on your knees and thank God that your pecker doesn't swell up and get tender once a month."

"Hi, Lydia," I said weakly, slinking into my chair.

An androgynous waitron walked up, bearing menus and an

expression of arctic disapproval. Lydia turned her searchlight smile on him/her. "Bring us some wine, darlin', would you?"

"I've got the wine list right—"

"Oh, I wouldn't know the difference. You California people and your wines. Just make sure it's nice and white and dry and *expensive*. All right? We're having a party here and I'm not paying for any of it." She beamed at me. "Claudia says you're at the Beverly Hillshire. Very chichi-poo-poo!"

"Where is Claudia?"

"She's not coming. There was a problem with the new bathroom. I've got you all to myself tonight."

"Lovely," I said.

Lydia ordered baby greens with raspberry vinaigrette and Montrachet. I settled for garlic-tortilla soup. Fortunately, the wine arrived first. I needed it.

"Sorry to hear about you and Charlie," I told her, pouring a second glass.

"Oh, no worries. Poor Charlie's just having a little midlife *crise de foi*. It started when he bought a Miata last winter and started using Rogaine, which is growing the most uncanny simulation of pubic hair all over his bald spot. . . . Anyway, he comes home from work a couple of weeks ago and says that he thinks we need to separate for a while, just so he can *find himself*. Can you believe that? *Find himself*. And I said, 'Fine. I wasn't aware you were *misplaced*, but I'll pick up the *Times-Picayune* and start looking for an apartment tomorrow.' "

The waitron scooped up our empty plates and fled.

"Well, old Charlie turns white and says, 'Oh, no, don't worry, I'll move out.' To which I said, 'Sorry, Boudreaux, but you're not sticking me with the kids while you go off and play slam-the-ham with some stewardess. You can find yourself just as easily here as you could in some singles condo. So you stay with Teddy and Melinda, and I'll give you a call as soon as I get my new number.' He turned from white to green. I picked up his keys and drove off in his Miata, which is still sitting in long-term parking at the New Orleans airport, by the way. And here I am!" Lydia paused long enough for another sip of wine. "Mmm. Faboo. And how's your writing going?"

"Oh, it's fine. Nothing to speak of, really, but—"

"Nothing?" Lydia clutched imaginary pearls, miming horror. "You're writing the Felina Lopez story! Tell me about it. Don't leave anything out."

I winced. "How'd you hear? Claudia?"

"Hollywood Today! We get that out in Louisiana, too, you know. I couldn't believe it when I heard your name."

"Do your parents know?" I said hesitantly.

"Kieran, you make it sound like you're writing kiddie porn! I think it's exciting. I remember every minute of the Ash trial. I'm a true-crime hag from way back. Ash, O.J., Menendez, Jon-Benet. I'd be the first in line to buy your book, even if you weren't my brother-in-law. I'm your target audience."

"Lydia," I said slowly, "why do you go for that stuff?"

"What else is there to watch? Movies?"

"Well, yeah."

"Good Lord, Kieran. Don't be ridiculous. Hollywood gave up catering to anyone over puberty eons ago. They don't make a movie anymore unless they can turn it into a Happy Meal. Now the only place to watch good dramatic stories is Court

TV." She swatted my wrist playfully. "Now give me the scoop before I positively *implode* with anticipation."

There was no way out of it. I gave her a thumbnail of events, leaving out a few salient points. My temporary roommate, for one. Brooks Levin's phone calls, for two. Lydia listened, eyes gleaming.

"Don't sound so embarrassed, Kieran!"

"Lydia, it's sleazy and—"

"Of course it is! It's sleazy and it's cheap and it's just so Hollywood I could die. Not just Hollywood, but modern America—"

I was spared Lydia's theories on modern America by the waitron, who set down our entrees carefully. The *chef de cuisine* at The Restaurant was Hans-Peter Jungenhoffman, the famed twenty-one-year-old wunderkind. Hans-Peter had a thing for vertical food; Lydia's tournedos of ostrich were sitting erect in a puddle of squid-ink pasta. Even my two shanks of osso buco were propped up over a haystack of *pommes frites,* leaning against each other like a pair of exhausted marathon dancers.

"The buzz on the Internet is that she was murdered," said Lydia.

"Of course she was."

"Not in a robbery. She had the goods on Dick Mann and was going to blab them all over town."

"I don't think so," I told her, slicing into my osso buco. "There was nothing in that manuscript worth killing over. She loved Dick Mann."

Lydia smirked. "Some people are even theorizing that she's still alive."

"What?"

"That her death was all some kind of publicity stunt for the book."

I put down my fork, astonished. "Lydia, where are you getting this stuff?"

"My newsgroup on the Internet. It's called alt dot true-crime. There's another theory that—"

"Lydia, any nutjob with a computer can post things on the Internet. Felina still alive? God. Next you'll tell me that she was seen working at an IHOP in Toledo with Elvis."

"So you don't think she was killed for something she knew?"

"Of course not. Do you?"

"Absolutely."

"Why?"

"Good Lord, Kieran. It's obvious someone doesn't want this book written."

So I'd gotten a phone call. So somebody didn't want this book written. That didn't mean Felina had been murdered, did it? She loved Dick Mann, didn't she?

A frisson tickled my spine, but I tore into my osso buco and ignored it. What did a bunch of Internet conspiracy theorists know, anyway?

Lydia insisted on dessert and liqueurs, which sent Charlie's bill to $214 with tip. When I got back, stuffed, my roomie was curled up on the sofa, snacking from a room-service tray of chocolate-covered fruit. Danziger was going to kill me when he got the bill.

Sloan looked up at me unenthusiastically and managed a "Hi."

". . . and no trip to Beverly Hills is complete without shopping," said the TV. "With literally hundreds of stores within walking distance, the Beverly Hillshire is the choice for—"

I snapped it off. "We have to talk, Sloan."

"About what?"

"For starters, about why I have to go down to the lobby every time I have to pee."

"Hey, it's not my fault that—"

"Sloan, I really don't give a hang. *This*"—I waved my copies of *Mann's Woman*—"is all that's on my mind right now."

"I clear out of here for most of the day, don't I? I leave you alone, don't I?"

"I don't *want* you to leave me alone. I want you to sit down and tell me everything you know about Felina Lopez. Tonight."

"I've told you everything I can think of."

"Sloan, this isn't just about the book. I'm also trying to find out why Brooks Levin is tailing us."

"I told you! I don't remember anything about her!"

"You certainly didn't have that problem with *Celeb*," I pointed out. "Your repressed memory syndrome seems to come and go."

She looked up at me blankly. Along with irony, sarcasm wasn't her strong point either. "Go ahead and get yourself something to drink. Make yourself comfortable. Because we are going to sit here, just you and me, and I am going to ask you questions, and I am going to *tweeze* those Felina memories out of your head, one by one. And if you don't like it, you can take your ass home right now."

She stomped into the bedroom and slammed the door.

"You better be packing in there."

Sloan slammed around in the bedroom for a minute, and then she came back into the living room and got an eight-dollar Japanese beer out of the minibar.

"We weren't friends. I mean, we worked for the same service, but we weren't girlfriends. I didn't even like her, really."

"But you did work together sometimes. You said that in your TV interview."

"A couple of times."

"Um . . . how does that work?"

She shrugged. "Client calls, says he wants two girls."

"What, like ordering two pizzas? Pepperoni and mushroom, blonde and redhead?"

"You're real funny. Like I said, we weren't friends. I really didn't—"

"Sloan, I saw your interview on *Hollywood Today!* You made it sound like you were friends."

"*They* made it sound that way. You know how they can twist stuff when they edit it."

I conceded the point. "Did she ever mention her family?"

"No."

"Father? Mother? Brothers or sisters?"

"Nothing. No. Not that I— Wait." Sloan looked genuinely surprised. "Her mother was dead. I do remember that."

"Did she mention anything about her dad?"

"I remember now. Her mother had died when she was very young. She was raised by her dad."

"She told you that?"

"No. We were at a party in Malibu. I remember her saying it to . . . to someone."

"Who was she talking to?"

"Oh, yeah, like I'm gonna give *you* the names of our clients."

"Did you know if they came to the U.S. legally?"

"I don't think so."

"How do you know?"

"I don't know . . . I just know that they didn't."

"Was her father's name Eduardo?"

"That sounds . . . yes! Yes!" She gaped at me as if I were a psychic. "That's right! I didn't remember that! How did you know?"

I squeezed her wrist. "Keep going! What else do you remember?"

It was like drawing a shade. Sloan's face clouded. "Nothing. I'm surprised I remember that much. Gimme a break." She slugged down the last of her beer. "Are we done?"

"Sloan, come on. You're doing great here."

"I told you. I didn't know her, and I didn't want to. Felina was a bitch. Put that in your book."

"Why was she a bitch?"

"Because. Because she sucked up to everybody who could do something for her. If you couldn't do something for her, then she didn't even pretend to be nice or even polite. It paid off. The agency would get these blind calls. If it was somebody well-connected or rich, if there was a big tip involved, Felina would get the call. If it was just some Cleveland in town with a room at the Ramada, it would go to me or somebody else. Somebody who wasn't the agency's pet."

I looked at Sloan, sitting there with no makeup and her chipped French manicure, and I thought of Felina's cheekbones, her long legs in the stovepipe jeans. Sloan was younger than Felina, but she probably didn't have more than two more years left. Felina could've still been working.

"Felina was a hypocrite," she added. "And I hate hypocrites."

"How?"

"She was a health-food nut. She had a hissy if anyone lit a cigarette around her. At the same time, she's going out with Dr. Pharmacy, Vernon Ash."

"Did you know Vernon?"

"Everyone knew Vernon. I mean, I met him. He was always around." She glared at me. "I don't do drugs, if that's what you mean. Never have, never will."

"Felina did, though."

"Yeah. She even went to Betty Ford for a while. Somebody else paid for it, of course."

"Who?"

"I don't know. Some rich guy. Well, a month after she gets out, I'm at a party in Laurel Canyon and I see her in the bedroom with Vernon, doing coke. And she was *pregnant*!"

"She was pregnant?"

"Sure. Good Catholic girls don't use a diaphragm or the Pill. They just get abortions or give the kids away." My poker face must have failed me, because Sloan sneered. "Don't give me that look. If I got pregnant, I could *never* kill my baby. I might not be Mother Teresa, but I damn sure ain't a hypocrite like Felina. Or you."

I put my chin in my hand and stared back at her tiredly. "Why am I a hypocrite, Sloan?"

"Give me a break. Look who *you're* in bed with. Felina sold out Vernon the minute she met Dick Mann and the D.A. offered to cut her a deal. Then she moved down to Mexico and became the Virgin Felina—'Oh, Hollywood's such a *bad* place, such an *evil* place.' You're both whores. The difference is that you're just a bad one."

"Screw it, Sloan. It's late, I'm tired, and I've got to be up early tomorrow to interview Betty Mann." I stood up. "And you're sitting on my bed."

"I'll be out of your way tomorrow. I'd rather take my chances with Brooks Levin than have to put up with your condescending attitude."

She stalked into the bedroom and slammed the door.

"You can get a cab tonight, as far as I care," I yelled.

No response.

I was too tired to argue. Tomorrow was going to be a long day.

= 10 =

HOTEL COUCHES ARE MEANT for writing postcards, not sleeping. At six I'd had enough. It was still dark outside, but I went up to the health club and sat in the whirlpool for an hour. It was so early that I had the place to myself, except for a couple of Japanese businessmen who padded through in towels and zoris.

It wasn't just my back that had kept me awake; it was the prospect of facing Betty Bradford Mann. Did the tab reporters still have those twinges of conscience, or did those nice fat paychecks massage away their qualms? And once I'd run that professional gauntlet, there was still the personal one: Tonight was the opening of Canem. Small talk with Claudia's parents would lead inevitably to the question of what I was writing these days. It was a tricky situation even without the nitroglycerin presence of Lydia, who seemed to contract Tourette's whenever she had an audience.

I took a quick sauna and a long cool shower before going upstairs to get dressed. I was supposed to be on the set at ten to meet Betty Bradford Mann and Susan D'Andrea.

Sloan still wasn't up. Surprise, surprise. I put on a nice Perry Ellis shirt, slacks, and a plain blazer. The blazer was in the front closet, crushed to one side by Sloan's outfits, and while I was digging it out, I noticed the floor safe. It seemed like a good place to keep my work, so I stowed my laptop and a copy of *Mann's Woman* in it. The other one I took with me so I could Fed Ex it to Jocelyn.

On the way out, I took the DO NOT DISTURB sign and reversed it. On the back it said: MAID CLEAN ROOM AS SOON AS POSSIBLE.

Just a little parting gift for my roommate.

Tourists are always surprised to find that they don't actually shoot movies in Hollywood. They used to, back in the age of the silents, but lack of space and cheap real estate sent most of the soundstages out to the San Fernando Valley and beyond. Hollywood the city was now one of those perennial urban-renewal areas that never quite gets renewed.

I was headed to a lot in Studio City, just off Ventura Boulevard. Trekking out to the Valley on a summer weekday is usually hell, with overheated cars and their overheated drivers lining the sides of the freeway, so I left early, cranked up the A/C and KROQ, and said a quick prayer before I got on the 101.

It worked; I pulled up at the studio gate with half an hour to spare. The guard found my name on the list, slapped a parking pass on my dashboard, and directed me to Stage 10.

Like every other lot, this one was a collection of numbered beige hangars with people in golf carts scooting between them like pinballs. The studio had installed speed bumps every few feet to keep real cars from mowing down the golf carts.

There was even an empty parking spot outside Stage 10 with VISITOR on it instead of the name of some executive. I pulled right in. "Doris Day parking," Claudia called it, after all those old movies where Doris would find a spot right in front of wherever she was going. I hoped that Doris Day parking was a good omen.

A placard on the door of Stage 10 announced that this was the set of *Miracle Over Atlanta: The Lucille Simon Story*. Lucille Simon had been in the news a few months back; she was a flight attendant who had saved a planeload of passengers after a mechanical failure. It made me think of Vernon Ash's book and the covers on Jack Danziger's walls. Whatever happened to original stories? Were there any titles left that didn't have a colon in the middle of them?

Inside the hangar it was dark and cool. I picked my way over a mole's nest of cables. All the action was at the other end of the cavern, through a thicket of Panavision cameras, gaffs, booms, and other equipment. At the center of all the fuss, on a platform, was the interior of an airplane. Not a whole airplane, but a 727 mock-up sliced in half from nose to tail. Behind the plane was a blue cyclorama. A faux-ceiling curved up over the whole thing, arching up in a way where the whole set could be lit from outside. The platform was mounted on a system of rollers and mechanical balances, to simulate choppy weather and mechanical failure.

Some people scurried around, but most were standing around in packs or slouched in canvas chairs, taking five. Caterers—*craft services,* in Hollywoodspeak—were laying out a spread on a long white table. I approached a harried-looking woman and introduced myself. She scurried away and returned with a Dockers-clad guy who stuck out his hand and said, "Darren Li. I'm the unit publicist on *Miracle*."

"Kieran O'Connor," I said, trying not to snicker. Having a publicist named Li was like having a dentist named Drill, or a proctologist named Butts.

"Kieran, Kieran, sure. I was just reading your column the other day. The one about the . . ."

"Party?"

"That's the one. So Susan tells me you're here to powwow with Betty. She's not ready yet, so you're stuck with me for a while, ha-ha. Hey, it's too bad you couldn't come on Friday. The real Lucille Simon is coming to meet Betty, and—"

"I'll take over from here, Darren," said a brisk voice.

A lot has been said in Hollywood about Susan D'Andrea's legendary harridanism—most of it in whispers. She was famous for not returning calls, screaming obscenities at reporters, and having more assistants quit than any other publicist in town. If Leo Lazarnick was the Nazi Paparazzi, Susan D'Andrea was the Flack Fatale.

"You'll be talking to Betty when they break for lunch, in her trailer." She looked around, as if there might be a shelf where she could put me. "I guess you could sit over there," she decided, pointing to a corner where a couple dozen extras were taking a break. "I'll come get you when Betty's ready, so don't wander away. *And don't talk to anyone.*"

"*Ja wohl,*" I said cheerfully, and wandered off to my corner.

A couple dozen members of the Screen Extras Guild— *atmosphere*—were chilling out between takes. Though they ranged from teenagers to seniors and wore everything from business suits to jogging outfits, all of them had a certain studied blandness. Distinctive looks spelled career doom to a professional extra. And these *were* professionals; most of them had brought their own directors' chairs, along with Game Boys, knitting, word-search puzzles, even a laptop or two. I maneuvered through the crowd until I found an open spot next to a heavyset fiftyish woman. Her name was Magic Markered on the canvas back of her chair: PEG SCHUCKETT.

I sat down on the floor next to Peg Schuckett and she started chatting away. "We'll be up and going again in a few minutes." Whispering: "Roger Dahlgren is in his trailer. I hear he's being difficult."

"Roger Dahlgren is in this?"

She gave me a funny look. "He's the pilot. Where have you been, dear?"

Peg Schuckett, it turned out, had been in more than two hundred movies and television shows, and remembered most of the titles. "You might remember me from this," she said, handing me a well-worn copy of *Biz*. "The page with the paper clip."

It was a one-sixteenth-page ad with a photo of Peg wearing a waitress's cap. PEG SCHUCKETT, TONIGHT ON *SEINFELD*, was the caption, along with contact information for some small-time agent out in Van Nuys. "Got a part opposite Valerie Bertinelli with that ad."

"So what's Betty Bradford Mann like?"

"Oh, very professional. I don't know. She doesn't go out of her way to talk to the extras, but she's nice enough." Her voice lowered again. "Of course, you know about the trouble she's had, poor thing."

Peg was about to give me the extras' poop on Betty Bradford Mann when an A.D. came over and told us, "That's it. We'll pick up after lunch, people."

I saw Susan D'Andrea steaming toward me. "There you are," she said sourly. "Let's do it."

A chubby young woman met us at the door of Betty's trailer. She carried two craft-services plates of sliced fruit: kiwis, mangoes, pineapple. "Hi, I'm Lesley," she said. "C'mon in. Betty's changing."

The trailer was pleasant but not particularly luxurious. It was furnished in soft peaches and purples, with a small sitting area, a makeup table, and a large desk. On the desk was a stack of eight-by-ten publicity glossies of the star, along with a few magazines and a PowerBook of considerably more recent vintage than my own.

Lesley sat the fruit down on the coffee table and knocked on a closed door. "Your lunch is here. So is your twelve o'clock."

"Okay," came a familiar voice. "I'll be out in a sec."

"Richie, you want a Coke or something?"

The head of a small boy poked out from around the sofa for a second before disappearing again.

"Come on out and say hi," said Lesley.

Nothing.

"Come on, Richie."

Slowly, a kid emerged: a thicket of ebony hair, sloe eyes, and bony legs sticking out of a pair of shorts. He wore an absurdly large pair of yellow basketball sneakers that made his feet look like Donald Duck's. A green Tonka was clutched in his fist.

I never know what to say to kids. I settled for, "Hi. I'm Kieran."

Silence.

Lesley made a what-can-you-do face at me. "Come on, Richie. You're a big boy. Say hi to Kieran."

Richie regarded me with kindergarten solemnity. "Hi. I'm *Rich*," he said, with a pointed look at Lesley.

"Rich, you big silly! Aren't you going to say hi?" Susan D'Andrea's voice was stickier than a Gummi Bear. "You remember me!"

With the most exquisite timing and only the slightest trace of condescension, Richie managed a singsong, "Hel-lo, Susan."

I tried not to grin. The enemy of my enemy is my friend.

The bathroom door opened and out came Betty Mann, wearing a terry robe over a flight attendant's uniform.

I compared her to the publicity glossies on her desk, and the juxtaposition was not flattering. She was either a good-looking forty-five or a well-preserved fifty. Smoker's cobwebs creased the corners of her lips. The face was reasonably tight, but her neck was stringy and the skin on her hands was like tissue. Plastic surgeons still haven't mastered necks and hands, and the first one who does is going to make a fortune.

Susan made the introductions. Betty shook my hand absently. "Did you get any lunch?" she asked her son.

"I thought maybe me and Lesley could go *out* for lunch."

Lesley and Betty exchanged a glance that I couldn't quite decipher. "Fine by me," said Lesley. "If your mom says so."

"I think I want some pesto." In the mouth of another kid, it might have sounded spoiled or precocious, but Richie said it like a tiny adult, just expressing a preference.

Betty still looked surprised. "Well . . . I don't see why not. You've been very good all morning." She grinned, and for a moment the creases in her face were laugh lines.

"Yes, definitely pesto," Richie decided. "California Pizza Kitchen would be good."

"Sounds fine to me." Lesley picked up her car keys. "We'll be back in a couple, Betty. I'll get your dry cleaning on the way back."

"Okay. Give me a hug, bug."

Richie gave his mother a quick one around the neck, the Tonka never leaving his fist, and headed out the door of the trailer.

"Richie! Say good-bye to everyone."

"Bye." He bunny-hopped down the steps, making as much noise as possible with his sneakers.

"Cute kid," I said.

Betty ignored me. "Why don't you get yourself some lunch, too, Susan?"

For once, Susan D'Andrea was at a loss for words. "Betty, I . . . I really think—"

"Thanks, but we'll be fine. Go eat."

"*Betty* . . ." Susan wheedled, in the tone of a defense attorney telling a client to *shut up*, "I *really* think it would be *best* if I—"

"*Susan*. We'll call you if we need you."

As the door closed, Susan shot me a look that reminded me of one of those cobras that could spit poison out of its eyes. Too bad there weren't any other reporters here to enjoy it. I'd be dining out for weeks on the tale of Susan D'Andrea's public spaying.

When we were finally alone, Betty sat down on a taboret across from me. She took a pack of Merits and a lighter from the pocket of the robe. I got out my microcassette.

"He's got quite a vocabulary. How old is he?"

"Six. Six at the end of September." She exhaled smoke from her nostrils dragon-style.

"Kindergarten or first grade?"

"Richie *was* in kindergarten. He's been having trouble sleeping lately. The doctor decided we should hold him back half a year."

I didn't say anything.

"Last time he was in school, he did a . . . he had a bowel movement. In class."

"I'm sorry. That's terrible. Poor guy."

"He gets hysterical if I leave the house." She wasn't even speaking to me anymore, just talking out loud. "If I can get him to eat once a day, it's a victory. I'm shocked he wanted to go to lunch with Lesley. Maybe it's a sign. Maybe he's doing better, and we can . . . get back to . . . get him back in . . ."

"Thank you for meeting with me," I said, trying to find a subtle way to steer the conversation to our topic.

"You could have left that tape recorder at home, you know. I'm not going to give you any interview."

I slipped the microcassette into my blazer pocket. "We can make it off the record."

"To hell with off the record. How about we just talk."

"Okay."

I waited. She looked at me, puffed her cigarette, and looked away again.

"Why are you doing this?"

"Doing—"

"This book. About my family. Don't answer that. It's obvious. For the money, right?" Her voice wasn't accusatory, just dead-dry. "No . . . don't answer that either. Of course you are. That's why people do anything. That's why I'm doing this movie. That's why Lesley's taking Richie to the Pizza Kitchen. That's why Susan didn't want to leave. Because we all get paid. Because of money." She laughed, a harsh bark. "What's that song from *Cabaret*? 'Mon-ey makes the world go around, the world go around . . .' "

"I'm not out to hurt you, Ms. Mann."

Betty snorted. "We all have jobs to do. Every single one of us. But you know something?"

She took a long hit off her cigarette and ground it out.

"I think *your* job is really, really, *really* shitty."

I didn't say anything.

"I never had any intention of giving you an interview. I just wanted to meet you." Betty lit another cigarette and turned on her ashtray, one of those smoke-eater models that gives off a low whine. "And I wanted you to meet me. I wanted you to see that this person you're writing about—this name that sells the tabloids and the books, this *celebrity*—is a flesh-and-blood person just like you."

Call me cynical, but the speech seemed a little rehearsed. The emotions were real enough, but actors have a way of performing without even realizing it.

"I'm not writing a book about you, Ms. Mann. I'm writing a book from Felina Lopez's notes."

"Which would not be of any interest to anyone, and which would not be published by anyone, if it weren't for her involvement with my husband." Now she was a starchy lawyer on a nighttime drama. "Conceded?"

"Conceded."

Her eyes flicked down to my left hand. "Married?"

I looked at the claddagh ring on my second finger, the ring that matched Claudia's. "No."

"Engaged?"

"Let's say involved."

"Involved. I love that word. It's a way of being committed without committing."

"Ms. Mann—"

"Skip it. So you're involved. Let's say your—girlfriend or boyfriend?"

"Girlfriend."

"Your girlfriend made a mistake. Had an affair. The two of you worked it out between yourselves. It was a brief unhappy moment in a long, happy life together. Then someone decided to make the whole mess public, years afterward. How would you feel?"

"I wouldn't feel very good at all."

"How would you feel if reporters were going through your garbage, looking to make up stories? Because that's happened, too. My husband wasn't dead two weeks, and I had tabloid jackals going through my garbage cans. What was I supposed to do, put on a wig and dark glasses and drive the stuff to the dump myself?"

Starchy Lawyer had been replaced by Wrongly Accused. "Ms. Mann, you and your husband—"

"So I sent Lesley to Adray's to buy a paper shredder. I even had her take the shredded stuff home with her and put it in *her* trash can. And they still came back. You know what horrible secret they found this time? A box of *Ding Dongs*. I'd bought them trying to get Richie to eat *something*. And the next Monday, I'm on the front page of *Celeb*: 'Grieving TV Star on Wild Eating Binge.' "

"Ms. Mann," I said, "like it or not, you and your husband are public figures."

"And that entitles you to go through my trash cans?"

"I didn't do that, did I?"

"You met my son. Is he a public figure? Even if he was, does that excuse you from human decency? Prince William lost his mother because of people like you."

I didn't say anything. The ashtray whined like a mosquito.

"I'm scared for him," she said quietly. "No. Scratch scared. Terrified. Because of what happened to you-know-who."

The star to whom she alluded was a sitcom queen and a staple in the tabloids. A tabloid reporter had called child protective services, posing as a neighbor, claiming the star was beating her ten-year-old son. It was a lie, but the agency was bound by law to check it out. And the tab got its story: The star was being investigated for child abuse.

"Is it fair that I can't take Richie to Gelson's because I don't want him to go through the checkout line and see the garbage that you people have written?"

"I don't work for the tabloids. And I don't think he's old enough to—"

"Oh, he's old enough. Old enough to be sucking his thumb and wetting his pants again. He's old enough for *that*." She jabbed her cigarette into the ashtray.

Now I knew why I'd been invited. I was a stand-in for everyone who had been hounding her, for all the Frank Grassleys and Gina Guglielmellis of the world.

"First of all, I'm sorry for your troubles, but I haven't caused any of them. I really haven't. Second, I think that maybe your husband should have considered you and your son before he got involved with Felina Lopez."

"My son wasn't even *born* then!" The contempt in her voice was acrid. "I don't blame Dick for this. I settled that in my mind a long time ago. I don't even blame Felina Lopez. It's you tabloid people who—"

"I'll repeat myself. I'm not a tabloid reporter."

"No. You're not. You're worse."

"How am I worse, Ms. Mann?"

"Because the tabloids go off the rack in a week. What you're doing is going to sit in bookstores for months. And it's going to be the one thing people remember about me and my husband."

"You're wrong. People don't remember these things."

She shook her head. "What's the first thing you think of when you think of Liberace?"

"Las Vegas."

"Bull. You think two things: *gay* and *AIDS*."

"Being gay and having AIDS are nothing to be ashamed of."

"Of course they're not. My point is, the man entertained millions of people for fifty years, and you still think *gay* and *AIDS*. None of what he accomplished matters. And ten years from now, the name Dick Mann will come up and the first thing they'll think of is *drugs* and *whores*. Because of your book."

She seized my arm. "There is a child here. A little boy. A little boy whose father made some mistakes. And now his father isn't here anymore. Isn't that enough for any five-year-old to bear? Do you have to make it worse?"

The ashtray hummed. I waited for her to continue, but she

wasn't speaking hypothetically now. She really wanted an answer.

". . . I don't know what to tell you."

Betty looked at me as if she were examining a sample under a microscope. "Of course you don't. Just do me this. You think of that little boy's face when you're writing."

She dropped my hand.

"All right. I want to have my lunch now. I think we're finished here."

I stood up and gathered my things, waiting to see if she said good-bye, but she was eating a slice of pineapple as if I'd left a long time ago.

11

WHEN I GOT BACK to the Hillshire, all I could think about was another shower. I felt grody, and it wasn't just the Valley heat and the smog. I wanted some time to myself before seeing the Dubuissons, and I was in the perfect frame of mind to evict a certain nonpaying houseguest.

But the room was quiet. Not a room-service cart to be seen. A maid had been in to make up my pallet on the sofa. The bedroom door was closed, but the French doors to the balcony had been left open and the curtains were fluttering.

"Sloan?"

No answer.

Good.

I pulled off my tie and sat down on the sofa. There were two messages on the voice mail, and I pressed the button as I pulled off my tie and sat down on the sofa.

"K-man, it's Jack." I could picture him leaning back in his ergonomic chair, hairy knuckles laced behind his head, talking into the headset that all the Hollywood bigwigs wore. "Just wanted to see how your meeting with Betty went. How's the book coming? I'd love an early look. I've got a dinner and a screening tonight, so try to get back to me before four-thirty. Talk to you."

K-man? I made a mental note to call him the Jackster next time we met. Message two clicked in.

"Hey, it's Lazarnick. Call me." *Click.*

Dialing, I wondered what that fat toad wanted. I hadn't even mentioned the nude photos to Jack Danziger, much less brought up the idea of buying them for the book. It would be my pleasure to tell the Nazi Paparazzi we would give him a pass.

He picked up on the first ring.

"It's Kieran O'Connor."

"Hey. Just called to gloat. You snooze, you lose."

"What are you talking about?"

"You haven't seen *Biz* yet? What the fuck kind of reporter are you?"

"I don't know. What kind of photographer are you, Leo?"

"Go pick up *Biz* and you'll see what kind of photographer I am." Lazarnick laughed. "You snoozed and you losed. Nice doing business with you, chump."

Click.

The Beverly Hillshire newsstand displayed *Biz* and the other industry dailies right next to *The New York Times* and my own paper. There was nothing Felina-related on the front page. I bought it and took it upstairs.

I found Leo's item buried on page 16, in the "Mag BIZ" column:

The BIZ Insider has learned that fotog **Leo Lazarnick** has sold 20-year-old pix of **Felina Lopez** to the British magazine *Roué*. Sources say the pix are nude shots, taken when Lopez was a struggling teenage thesp. Sources at *Playhouse* and several American tabloids confirm that Lazarnick approached them last week with the pix. The asking price: $80,000.

Lopez, who was slain at her Mexican home earlier this month, became the center of a brief tabloid frenzy after it was revealed that **Jack Danziger** at Danziger Press was preparing an instatome about her life. The former prostitute had fled to Mexico after appearing as a witness in the **Vernon Ash** criminal trial.

Reached in London, *Roué* assistant editor **Colm Graham** would not comment. Lazarnick did not return phone calls.

Well, at least they left my name off this one.

I went into the bedroom and pulled off my shoes. Eighty thousand dollars for a few titty shots. I wasn't sure whose priorities were more screwed up: Lazarnick's, *Roué*'s, or the world's.

Or mine.

I peeled off my jacket and draped it over the suit tree for housekeeping. Sloan's bed had been made up as well, but the bathroom sink was still a hodgepodge of alpha-hydroxy this and seaweed-masque that. At least there was a fresh robe on the back of the door.

As I stepped into the shower, the sight of my body in the full-length mirror stopped me. I'd never been a fine physical specimen—Claudia once described me as "stocky but scrawny"—but the growing thickness around my waist had settled into a spare tire with some to spare. I used my fingers as calipers and found that I could pinch quite a bit more than an inch. Once this book was done, I should probably use some of my Danziger money to make a down payment on a membership at Le Sweat, or at least the Sixth Street Y.

I turned the water on full force and tried to wash off my encounter with Betty Bradford Mann.

My meeting with Betty. That's right; I'd forgotten something.

Fifteen minutes later, wrapped in a towel, I took my blazer off the suit tree. In the breast pocket was my microcassette recorder.

I removed it and pressed Rewind for a few seconds.

"—*ten years from now, the name Dick Mann will come up and the first thing they'll think of is drugs and whores. Because of—*"

I stopped it and popped out the tape. The microphone had been sensitive enough to pick up her voice, even through the lining of the blazer. I'd wondered about that as I'd slipped it into my pocket and pressed the Record button.

Standing there, staring at the little plastic rectangle, I knew why the tab reporters were paid the big bucks. Conscience costs.

It wasn't too late to redeem myself. All I had to do was disembowel the cassette, step out on the balcony, and unspool it like ticker tape all the way down to Wilshire Boulevard.

Even if I did, though, it was too late. I'd crossed a line that I never thought I'd approach, much less overstep.

I opened the closet and got down on my knees.

The safe popped open as if it had been waiting for me. The tape went in the back, under my laptop and next to my copy of the manuscript. I shut the door and gave the tumblers a spin before I went back and *thwupped* down on the bed. The room was dark and deliciously cool.

At the moment when I'd pressed the Record button, I'd told myself that it was just to help refresh my own memory, that I'd never obtain an interview with anyone under false pretenses, much less tape something that was supposed to be off the record.

But the book wasn't coming together.

And what Betty had to say would go a long way toward fixing it.

Besides, I told myself, what if I included her denouncement of the tabs? What if I put in her defense of Dick Mann, her plea to leave Richie alone? That might add another dimension to the story, beyond the world of sex and drugs, of Vernon Ash and Sloan Baker. It might fill out the picture. It might make people think. It might . . .

It might sell a lot more books.

I pressed my face into the clean pillow. A line from James Baldwin ran through my head:

There's always further to fall, always, always.

Someone as scummy as myself should have had more trouble sleeping. I was a log. By the time I woke up, I'd overslept by half an hour. By the time I got out to Venice and managed to find a parking spot, I was nearly an hour late. There wasn't a spot to be found within four blocks of Café Canem.

Walking up Abbot Kinney Boulevard, I could see the joint was packed; the front doors were open and zydeco music was blasting into the street. People were standing in clumps on the sidewalk, smoking, chatting, drinking lattes and macchiatos. Claudia's friend Dagny Weiss was checking invitations at the door, joking with the crowds and fending off the street people. Tonight Dagny was in Marlene Dietrich dominatrix mode, with a leather cap, vinyl bustier, black fishnets, and a pair of boots that laced all the way up to her hips. Ilsa, She-Wolf of West L.A.

She kissed my cheek. "Where've you been, stranger?"

"Working."

"Hear you got a book deal."

"I'll fill you in later," I mumbled. "I need to get in there and press the flesh."

"There's a lot of flesh to press."

It was unreal how many people were crammed into that small space. All the Hollywood parties in the world hadn't relieved my claustrophobia. I scooted toward the back, squeezing through neighbors, guests, and people I'd never seen before. Jeff Brenner and Karen Trujillo were perched on top of one of the washing machines. Jeff caught my eye and pantomimed strangulation. I nodded miserably.

Despite all the labor pains, Canem was a beautiful creation, a Tennessee Williams opium dream. Claudia had gotten rid of all her beloved kitsch and gone back to her New Orleans roots for inspiration. Subdued blue-green light shone from recessed fixtures, and candles flickered shadows on the brickwork. A bank of computer stations against the south wall made a blue glow. The trompe l'oeil window behind the service counter looked lush and mysterious, with silhouettes of banana trees and a gibbous moon hanging fat in the night sky. *Hush . . . Hush, Sweet Charlotte* was playing silently on the video monitors. Claudia's favorite, Zachary Richard, provided a tinny, cheerful soundtrack.

A vague pang hit somewhere around my breastbone. Once this would have been a joint project between the two of us, Claudia bouncing every obsessive detail off me until I gave in and got obsessed with the project myself. How had she managed to get so much done without me?

Obviously she'd managed just fine.

I wasn't sure what bothered me more: the fact that Claudia had managed so well on her own, or that I seemed to be flailing without her.

12

EVERYTHING WAS FREE TONIGHT, and the pastry case had been looted. I grabbed a cup and pumped the French roast carafe on the counter. Empty. Well, making coffee—that I could do. Not totally useless after all.

I stepped behind the counter and was grinding beans just as Claudia's parents walked up, arm in arm.

Chessy Soniat Dubuisson was a New Orleans Brahmin from an old Uptown family. Claudia told me she had been queen of one of the old-time Carnival krewes in her youth. Now she was a psychologist, and her husband was a pediatrician with a couple of offices around the city. I liked both Dr. Dubuissons and they were always exquisitely nice to me, but something about them made me feel vaguely disreputable and inadequate. Maybe it was their happy, well-fed, well-paid perfection. Or maybe I just can't handle shrinks.

"Hello, dear," her mother said.

"Hi, Dr. Dubuisson. Hi, Dr. Dubuisson. Can I get you anything?"

"Call me Chessy, dear." She was decked out in a smart business suit and her signature gold Mignon Faget jewelry. As always, her hair was neatly coiffed, soft and feminine, and her makeup was understated and perfect. She had all the poise of a beauty queen with none of the vulgarity.

"Claudia tells us you've been working on a book," said the other Dr. Dubuisson, the one with the walrus mustache and the pigeon-gray three-piece.

"Well, that I have. That I have," I chirped, feeling ridiculous. I rummaged under the counter and came up with a square white box. "Hey, look what I found. Croissants. Looks like chocolate and raspberry and—"

"What's it about?" Claudia's mother leaned forward with genuine interest.

"About?"

"The book, dear."

"Oh, it's a Hollywood thing." Where was this light voice coming from? "Didn't Claudia tell you anything about it?"

Dr. Dubuisson snorted. "We've barely seen her since we got here."

"Poor thing, she's been swamped," soothed Chessy.

"Somebody ought to tell that friend of hers he looks ridiculous."

"That's just Pedro."

Pedro was Claudia's best friend and the manager of Café Canem. He was half-Samoan, half-Mexican, one hundred percent gay, and two hundred percent exhibitionist. Claudia said he had been considered outrageous even in New Orleans, which was saying something. God only knew what he would wear to something as important as the opening night of Canem. He liked to dress for shock value, even though he was about as swishy as Mike Ditka.

"Where is Claudia?" I asked.

"She's out on the back patio talking to a crew from the local news."

Scratch the patio as an escape. "And where's Lydia?"

"Sitting on the back stairs with the little ones," said Chessy. "We brought them in as a surprise. I just came to get another cup of that wonderful Irish coffee for her."

"I'll take it to her."

"Relax, son, it's a party." Dr. Dubuisson grinned a grin that made me suspect there was more than just cream and sugar in his coffee.

"Yes, sir. I'm trying." I pumped a couple cups of Irish mocha and started to make my way to the back hallway.

Maneuvering through a packed crowd with two cups of scalding coffee takes some skill. I got stuck behind some jamoke with a ponytail who was trying to pick up a woman in a vintage strapless. Who were these people?

Wriggling through another conversational clot, I noticed Brenner and Karen sitting on the washing machine, and the sight stopped me dead.

I saw Jeff—really *saw* Jeff—for the first time in years.

He'd always been the good-looking one in our pack of friends. Brenner's face was still unwrinkled, his hair thick and wheaty, but there was something different there: a solidness about his features, like clay that had begun to harden. I stared, amazed at my perception. It was like putting on a new pair of glasses. Karen was different, too. I knew both Karens: the respected seismologist and the *real* Karen, the one who wore leather minis, got polluted on Jagermeister, and laughed at *Ren and Stimpy* reruns. But the grown-up woman sitting on the washing machine, splitting a plate of food with her husband, was the Earthquake Lady and no one else.

A pride of tattooed and pierced teenagers sulked its way past, jostling my coffee, and it hit me: Jeff and Karen looked more like the Doctors Dubuisson than they did the teenagers. Did I? No.

Did Claudia?

Lydia was perched on the back stairs, watching her kids try to catch chocolate-covered espresso beans in their mouths. The number of beans rolling around on the floor testified to their bad aim. "Kieran! Thank God," Lydia said, taking the coffee. "Melinda, Teddy, go in the front room and show your grand-mother how well you catch."

"Grandma told us not to do it," said Teddy, shooting me a sour look. Obviously I was the death of the party.

"Well, there's got to be a hundred people out there. Go find someone to show. I want to talk to Kieran." She clapped her hands. "*Allons-y.*"

Melinda and Teddy were polite enough to scoot away, and impolite enough to stick out their tongues at me as they left. Lydia pulled her dress away from her bodice and fanned herself. "Lord. That vasectomy we got Charlie three years ago was the best money we ever spent."

Lydia was wearing one of her usual dressed-to-thrill outfits, a neon-orange tunic with silk scarves in shades of yellow and magenta. The outfit was topped off with a pair of red alligator boots. God only knew what she wore to the grocery store.

"These people are a pack of bores. Except Pedro, of course.

I've been waiting for you all night. What's up with the Felina book?"

"Just interviews. I met with Betty Bradford Mann today."

Her eyes gleamed. "What was that like?"

"Oh, I was a whipping boy. A stand-in for all the tabloid reporters of the world." I didn't want to think about Betty Bradford Mann. "Where's Claudia?"

"Now, don't go looking for her just yet. I've got a few more questions for you."

We were interrupted by the crew from Channel 9, who walked in off the back patio. They were led by a man in a long white dress.

"Pedro, you and Dagny are the only ones here with any style," Lydia said. "Besides myself, of course."

Pedro did a supermodel spin, showing off his outfit. It looked like a Mexican girl's confirmation dress, if they made confirmation dresses that fit the Green Bay Packers. A foot-long crucifix hung around his neck by a bike chain. Years of exposure to Pedro Espinosa had rendered me unshockable. He would have to wear a polo shirt and a pair of Dockers to floor me.

"Claudia's wondering where you are," he informed me.

"I'll go get her."

Pedro hoisted his sails and steamed toward the main party. I started to stand, but Lydia pulled me back down again. "I said I'm not done with you yet."

"Lyd, I'm tired of talking about that damn book—"

"I don't want to talk about that. I want to talk about you and Miss Claudia Marie."

"What do you mean?"

"Kieran, what the heck is up with you two? You having problems?"

Other than the fact that we're barely speaking, going out of our way to avoid each other, and haven't had sex in months, everything's fine.

I didn't know what to say, so I stared at the floor. Claudia's new hexagonal black-and-white tile was littered with espresso beans, along with Hot Wheels and weensy haute couture outfits from some doll. Slut Barbie, by the looks of them. I decided to use an ancient trick favored by psychologists and reporters: turn the question around.

"Why would you say we're having problems?"

"Boo, I've been here almost a week, and Claudia has mentioned you exactly twice. Not only haven't you been down here helping, you haven't even been calling. Something must be going on if even self-centered old me has noticed it."

"We're *busy*, Lydia." I was getting irritated. "What do you want me to say?"

"You can tell me, *me cher*. I'm practically your sister-in-law. Are the two of you having problems? Do I need to intervene? Slap baby sister around a little bit? You're still wearing your ring, so what's the scoop?"

I stared at the claddagh on my finger.

Our rings had brought us nothing but trouble since I'd bought them on impulse six months before. At the time, Claudia and I had decided to wear matching claddagh rings—Irish wedding bands—and figure out the symbolism later. It seemed like a good idea then. They weren't wedding rings, obviously, and they certainly weren't friendship rings, but they weren't engagement rings, either. Neither one of us was quite clear exactly *what* they were.

"We're fine, Lydia, really. I mean, we're not heading for the altar or anything, but—"

"Well, for crying out loud, when are the two of you going to bite the bullet and do it? When you're collecting Social Security and still engaged?"

"Engaged? We're not engaged!"

Lydia stopped in mid-sip of her coffee, eyes aglitter. I started to stammer an explanation, but she clamped her hand over my mouth and shouted, "Claudia!"

Claudia came in from the patio, carrying a tray of cappuccino bowls with foamy edges. "Oh. You're finally here."

"Hey, Claude. You need any help?"

"No, everything's going fine, believe it or . . ."

She glanced at the mess of coffee beans on the floor, and then up at me. Her head pulled back a fraction of an inch. I felt it, too; the air was charged with emotional ozone.

What the hell is going on here? asked her eyebrows.

Don't ask me . . . she's your sister, my eyebrows replied.

Lydia was oblivious. "Claudia Marie, what is going on with you and Kieran?"

"What are you talking about?"

"Are you or are you not engaged?"

Claudia looked at me again. "Lydia," she said slowly, "what made you think we were engaged? Am I missing something here? Kieran, did you tell her that—"

"*No.*"

"Where did you get that idea, Lydia?"

"Well, *pardonnez* the fuck outta *moi*," said Lydia, "but when a man and a woman wear matching . . ."

Her voice dribbled away.

We both saw it at the same moment: Claudia's hand, holding the cappuccino tray, and the bare ring finger that curled around the top.

The hand dropped the tray.

Over the noise and the music, I heard something very big shatter, and then I was on my feet and heading for the front door.

I smashed into someone's back, getting a shirtful of lukewarm latte for my trouble, and flashing past my vision like a billboard on the highway was the face of Chessy Dubuisson, mouth in an O as big as Texas.

As I hit Beverly Hills, I made a California stop at a red and picked up a BHPD cruiser for my carelessness. It followed me down Gregory and up El Camino, cruising my tail like a patient shark, finally giving up when I turned into the porte cochere at the Beverly Hillshire. There was a mini traffic jam; a banquet was getting out and the porte cochere was clogged with cars. I put the car in park and exhaled. My shirt was ruined. I smelled like Juan Valdez and looked like the *Exxon Valdez*.

We weren't engaged. Never had been. We were—what?—involved.

Involved. I love that word. It's a way of being committed without committing.

Thank you, Betty Bradford Mann.

So why did I feel so devastated?

And yet, under everything, I felt a budding sense of relief.

Relief that one of us had finally taken our comatose relationship off its life-support system. For too long, we had been drifting apart unyoked, planets that have slowly left their mutual orbit. Now it was over. Fini.

"A relationship is like a car," Jeff Brenner told me once, "and it takes a hell of a lot of maintenance."

Well, I was never too good at maintenance on my car, either.

All I wanted to do now was finish the book, get my stuff out of Claudia's apartment, find a place to stay, and have Jocelyn pimp me out for another high-paying tell-all. And if Sloan was still upstairs, I'd kick her out physically if need be, by elevator or balcony.

A valet opened my door. I accepted the proffered claim ticket and was striding toward the door of the Hillshire when the whole side of the hotel lit up harsh and white as lightning.

A cameraman appeared. On the side of his videocam were the words *Hollywood Today!*

Frank Grassley materialized, grinning.

My first reaction was to run, curse, and flip him the bird, but I controlled myself. *That's what they want. You run, you look like you've got something to hide. Curse at him, flip him off, and they get their money shot.*

I stood. Smiled, even. It was like turning the wheel of the car in the direction of a skid—an act that made every synapse in my body scream.

"Evening, Frank," I said pleasantly. Behind him, I saw a man in a suit pointing at us, and two uniformed Hillshire security agents break into a trot. "Your hair looks especially lustrous tonight."

He couldn't be baited. "Kieran O'Connor," he said portentously, "word has it that you're hiding out here to escape the person who—"

Too late; the security guards were on him like Dobies. One of them blocked me and the shot with his body; the other wedged Frank against the wall of the building.

"Gentlemen, you must leave. This is private property. Failure to leave immediately will result in criminal prosecution."

"Word has it," yelled Frank, "that you're hiding out here to escape the person who murdered Felina Lopez. Can you tell us why—"

"This is private property. Failure to leave immediately will result in criminal prosecution."

The banquet crowd had frozen to watch this triumph of investigative journalism. I slipped inside as the guards began to hustle Frank down the porte cochere.

"Why won't you answer my question?" he shouted as they dragged him backward down the driveway.

I yelled back at the top of my lungs, "Frank, for the last time, I won't marry you. You're a swell guy, but I like women."

I walked into the hotel triumphantly. Riding up on the elevator, I felt good for the first time that night. Or that day.

The feeling lasted all of forty-five seconds, until I slipped the card key into the door of my room and turned on the light.

I stood in the doorway for a second, paralyzed, before taking two tentative steps inside.

Cushions were upended from the sofa. The minibar hung open. Drawers were scattered like blocks. Even my pillow had been removed from its case. The bedroom door was closed, but I was sure it had been trashed as well.

No. Not trashed. There was order to this disorder.

Someone had gone through my suite methodically, looking for something.

I'd heard burglary victims talk about feeling violated, and I finally understood what they meant. My hand even went to my groin for a second.

I checked the front closet. Sloan's clothes were still there. No; some of them were gone. Empty hangers hung askew. A few items had even fallen on the floor, as if someone had pulled the clothes off in a big hurry.

Under all the clothes on the closet floor was the safe, and the door was wide open.

THREE

= 13 =

IF IT WAS A Betty Bradford Mann TV movie, it would have
been called *Terror on the 34th Floor: Break-In in Beverly Hills*. By
the time hotel security and the BHPD got there, our group had
gotten so large we had to move from the manager's office to a
conference room on the second floor of the hotel. Dramatis
personae included me; the hotel's night manager; the head of
security; some Hillshire functionaries of unknown origin; and
four Beverly Hills cops, only two of whom ever spoke.

After they had me write a list of everything that was missing, they passed it off to yet another cop and plopped me in a
gold banquet-room chair. One of the hotel functionaries got
me a glass of water with a lemon slice in it. It felt more like a
press conference than an interrogation. I cleared my throat,
drank my water, and told them everything. Almost everything.

My trip to Mexico. Felina's murder. The book deal. The
threatening phone call at the Wind & Sea. My meeting with
Sloan Baker, Vernon Ash, Leo Lazarnick, and Betty Bradford
Mann. Sloan's identical phone call. Sloan moving in. Getting
ambushed by Frank Grassley. Going upstairs and finding my
room trashed and Sloan gone. The cops took notes, grunting a
question here and there.

"Who knew you were staying here?" asked the cop in charge. Most of the BHPD are impressive specimens, but this one could have moonlighted at Chippendales. His uniform looked like a breakaway costume, with a leather vest and G-string underneath.

"Nobody, really. Just the people who were working on the book with me. My agent, Jocelyn, but she's in New York—"

"Go through them one by one. Last names, too."

"Jocelyn Albarian." I spelled it. "Kitty Keyes was Felina's agent. My publisher, Jack Danziger. My girlfriend, Claudia Dubuisson. Oh, and her sister. Lydia Boudreaux."

"And the Baker woman."

"Yeah. Sloan Baker."

"And the people you interviewed." He checked his notes. "Leo Lazarnick, Vernon Ash, Betty Bradford Mann."

"No. They had my phone number, but they didn't know where I was staying. That number didn't ring through the hotel switchboard."

"We change it after each guest leaves," said the night manager.

"Somebody could've traced it, I guess," I said.

"Possibly," said Officer Chippendales. "But quite a few people already knew where you were staying. Not to mention the guy from *Hollywood Today!*"

"*Hollywood Today!*" moaned the night manager. Apparently the Visigoths would have been more welcome.

"Hey, I didn't tell him where I was," I said. "Somebody must have tipped him off. Believe me, I don't talk to those types."

The silent cops exchanged smirks. Dummy. I *was* one of those types.

"That threatening phone call you claimed you got," said Chippendales. "Any idea who that might have been?"

"I didn't recognize the voice."

"Any guesses?"

There was a large ashtray next to me, with a BH crest stamped in the sand. I dragged my finger through it.

"Couldn't even hazard a guess."

I'm a terrible liar. But Officer Chippendales just shrugged and made another note. "You don't have *any* idea who could have done this?"

"Nope." Another lie. This was professional work, and the whole tableau pointed to only one professional.

I still didn't know what Brooks Levin wanted, but if he was capable of tracking both Sloan and me down, he was certainly capable of breaking into a hotel room at the Beverly Hillshire and cracking a safe. God only knew what else he was capable of.

The image of Felina's body leaving the beach house flashed in my head. I took another sip of water.

This was serious, and it was time I started taking it seriously.

"Can I make a phone call, please?"

The night manager looked horrified. "You don't need to call a lawyer, Mr. O'Connor."

"I don't want a lawyer. I want my agent."

The cops smirked at each other again.

"Just say the word and I'll be on a plane out there immediately," said Jocelyn. "I could be in Beverly Hills by mid-afternoon."

I slouched on Jack Danziger's sofa, sipping coffee from a Fiestaware mug and tracing patterns in the carpet with my toe.

The coffee was cold. It was six in the morning, and the adrenaline was finally beginning to drip out of my limbs. Tired and wired had been battling in my body for hours, and tired was starting to win.

I cradled the receiver under my chin. "Why?"

"Because I'm worried, Peaches."

"Don't worry. The police said whoever it was wasn't after me, just the manuscript. I'll have to find another hideout, that's all."

"Kieran—"

"Jocelyn, you can worry about me in New York just as well. They got one copy of the manuscript, but the one I was going to send to you was still in my car. Believe me, everything's okay. I'm just a little shaken up."

"I'm not worried about the manuscript, idiot child, I'm worried about *you*."

Kitty Keyes drifted into the living room, blowing on her own cup of coffee. Her hair was blowsy and the bags under her eyes hung like crepe. She didn't look like a Mary Kay lady anymore, just a tired old woman in a Little Orphan Annie hairstyle.

"Kitty just got here."

"Let me talk to her. Is Jack available yet?"

"No. He's still in the kitchen, talking to the police."

"Fine. Now give Kitty the phone and go get some sleep."

I surrendered the phone and paced the living room aimlessly.

Jack Danziger might have been a sleaze merchant, but he'd recycled his lucre. No zebra-skin rugs or gold-leaf pool tables here. The room was masculine, with a refined eye, accented with good heavy furniture and a couple of reproduction Hepplewhite chairs. At least I assumed they were reproductions. If they weren't, I wouldn't plant my butt on them for fear of snapping off a leg.

A baby grand was topped with fresh flowers and some framed photos, mostly candid shots of Danziger with his friends: skiing, sailing, Oscar night at Dani Janssen's house. A few of the shots were of beautiful women, Danziger's hand invariably slipped around one smooth hip. One of the women—a bowl-cut blonde with an oversized chest—looked familiar, but I couldn't place her.

"No, I'm fine, we're all just a little upset . . . Mm-hm . . . Oh, that won't be necess— Oh, I know, we're all concerned about that . . . Of course not . . ." Kitty patted a stray wisp of strawberry hair back into place absently. "No, I'm setting the whole thing up . . . That's right . . . Well, the hotel will, of course . . . Completely safe, I guarantee you . . . All right, I'll have him call you as soon as he's done with the police. Good-bye, dear."

"Sorry to get you over here so early in the morning," I told her.

"Oh, please. Once the police called, I wouldn't have been able to get back to sleep. I usually don't get any more than four hours a night, anyway. My husband used to tell me, 'Kitty, you're full of more p-and-v than a hummingbird.' " She sat down beside me. "How are you, dear?"

"Tired of that question more than anything."

"You look tuckered."

"Kitty, I don't know what I'm going to do next."

"Get some sleep, is what you're going to do. Don't worry, dear." She smoothed my hair. "Get some rest. We'll talk about it over lunch. I've taken care of the whole thing. And try not to think about it too much."

Right.

Jack Danziger's guest room was equipped with a bed that felt like God's own four-poster. Porthault sheets, a pile of marshmallowy pillows, and a quilted duvet with a six-inch loft. After Claudia's no-nonsense futon, the glorified army cot at the Wind & Sea, and the sofa at the Beverly Hillshire, I wanted just to lie there and enjoy it for a while, but I fell out as if I'd been drugged.

When I woke up again, it was eleven-fifteen and the room was flooded with light: one of those perfect clear-sky days that makes winter-weary New Englanders swear they're going to move to California. Birds chirped in the sycamores outside the window. Somewhere downstairs, a television was playing. I lay there for a few more minutes, savoring the very wombness of the bed. When I finally groaned my way out of the sheets, it was noon.

The clothes I'd worn to the opening of Café Canem, including my coffee-soaked shirt, were in a messy pile at the foot of the bed. I pulled them on and checked myself in the mirror over the bureau. I looked as rumpled as my shirt. Oh, well. I ran a few fingers through my hair, trying to tame the black Irish cowlicks, and padded downstairs barefoot.

No one was in the living room. The drapes had been pulled back on the picture window, revealing a U-shaped driveway, a stand of trees, a lawn so green it could have been dyed, and more prime Hancock Park real estate across the street.

And news vans.

Three of them. One had the familiar *Headline Journal* logo on the side. The other two were from the local news stations, with huge antennas on top wound with snaky neon-orange cable. One of the doors was open, and I could see a technician inside munching a sandwich, silhouetted against several TV screens.

My entourage. They were sticking to me like a case of the crabs. I followed the sound of the TV into a dining room and pushed open the swinging doors to the kitchen.

A woman in chef's whites was standing at a butcher-block island, chopping green peppers at the speed of light, guiding the knife with her knuckles. If I tried that, I'd end up with knuckles tartare. Several brown bags sat on the sinktop, next to a half-flat of strawberries that was waiting to be rinsed and hulled. She looked up from her chopping.

"Hi. I'm Kieran."

"Hey. I'm Elise. As in 'Für Elise.' Grab me the rest of the peppers, would you? They're in one of those bags." She grinned. "When Jack surprises me with an overnight guest, it's usually a woman."

The bags were heavy with summer fruits in riotous South Beach colors: plums, peaches, oranges. I found two cello bags of yellow and red peppers and brought them over.

Elise was only about twenty-three, but she was efficient, in a butch way. She used the end of her knife to scrape the green peppers into a neat pile and began chopping away at the yellow ones. "You looked outside yet?"

"Sorry about that."

"I drove up from the greenmarket this morning and felt like a movie star. Don't worry, they're not going to bother us. Jack called Southtec and they sent over a security car. There's two guards in the driveway, making sure they stay on public property. You're safe." She gave a pepper a whack with her knife, cleaving it into two perfect bells.

"Can I have a plum?"

"*May* I. But sure. Have whatever you want." She wrinkled her nose. "I'll find you a fresh shirt when I get done here."

I took my plum and sat down at the butcher-block island. The kitchen was as designer-perfect as the rest of the house. Wood floors, emerald marble countertops, and a two-basin stainless-steel sink deep enough to wash an Airedale. The cabinets were light wood with matching green marble pulls. The focus of the room, though, was a built-in wine cellar with a glass front. Hundreds of bottles were neatly racked with their necks pointing sixty degrees toward the floor. Gauges on the front controlled temperature and humidity. This is the house that Jack built, paid for by a million tell-alls.

"What are you making, Elise?"

"Three-pepper pasta. You don't cook the sauce. It's just yellow, green, and red peppers, mixed with vinaigrette and a little nonfat mozzarella. You pour the whole thing over bowtie pasta and add some fresh basil. Best thing you've ever tasted. You hungry?"

"A little. You think I could have some coffee first?"

"Jack doesn't drink coffee."

"Oh."

"But I do." She pointed to a French press on the stove. "Get yourself a mug and pop it in the microwave. Jack said he'd be home for lunch about one, one-thirty. You hungry now? There's a pitcher of yogurt smoothies in the fridge, or I could whip up an egg-white omelette."

"No, thanks. I can wait." I liked my omelettes with plenty of yolk, dripping with butter and melted cheese.

The microwave beeped. I took out my coffee and drifted around the kitchen for a minute, munching my plum and enjoying the clean, pungent smell of bell pepper.

One whole wall was hung with a collection of cleavers, whisks, and other professional equipment that looked straight out of the Williams-Sonoma catalog. I had no idea what most of them were designed for. On a low counter was a collection of oversized plastic vitamin-type bottles with names like Yohimbe, Whey Protein, Shark Cartilage 2000, and Protex Z-100. I read the back of one bottle. *Formulated with a blend of protein isolates and fractions chosen for high biological values, maximum amounts of BCAA's, high L-Arginine ratios, and excellent amino acid profiles.* Well, *that* cleared things up.

"How long have you worked for Jack?"

"About six months." She slid the tiny yellow squares off her chopping block into a stainless-steel bowl and started in on the red peppers. "He hired me and my partner to cater a party last winter. We've got a company, Movable Feasts. Then he offered me mucho dinero to come work for him. So Beth is running the catering firm while I cater to Jacko."

I flicked my plum stone into the garbage can. "He lives in this place all alone?"

"Yup." She laughed. "Beth told him that we'd cater his wedding for free."

"Jack's getting married?"

"Nah. It's never gonna happen. Jack's a dog. That's why she offered it." She grinned at me. "Hey, you want to grab a shower before he gets back? All the stuff is out at the pool house."

"Thanks."

Outside the back door was a pool so long it should have had mile markers on the sides. In the cabana was a dressing room and shower, complete with shampoo, conditioner, designer soaps, towels, even shaving cream and disposable razors. I took a long, lazy shower, scrubbing my scalp with peppermint-nettle shampoo and enjoying the sensation of having four shower-heads pelt me at the same time.

This wouldn't be a bad place to ride out the remainder of the book, with a pool in the backyard, a Southtec car in the drive, and Elise in the kitchen.

Money may not be able to buy happiness, but it sure gets you damn good water pressure.

When I padded back into the kitchen, wearing a pair of flip-flops from the cabana, Elise wasn't there. There was a fresh shirt draped over the back of a chair. I stripped mine off and put it on. Through the swinging doors, I heard Kitty and Jack.

". . . best place for him," Kitty was saying.

"It might work. It's going to be expensive, though. I swear, sometimes I wish I'd never cooked up this project."

"I know."

"No, Kitty, I mean it. If we hadn't dropped so much money so far, I'd have half a mind to cancel it. Never had a book give me so much trouble. Never."

"Don't worry, Jack. It'll be over soon. I figured out where we could put him."

First Jocelyn, now Kitty and Danziger. Was this what it was like to be a celebrity? People planning your life for you?

"Hi," I said brusquely, walking in. "So what's up?"

Jack and Kitty looked up guiltily. Elise was ladling pasta into three plates. Kitty had pulled herself into a semblance of her old self. Even Jack looked slightly rested, in a maroon polo shirt that showed off his biceps. "Hey, it's the media man," he said. "How you feeling, sport?"

"I'm sorry. I don't know how they found out I was here. Even if it's a slow news day, they should go away in a few hours."

"Don't worry. I've never had this much pre-publicity on a book before." Jack grinned.

"How are you feeling, dear?" Kitty asked.

"I'm okay. I slept good."

"Slept *well*," said Elise. "I got C's in English and I know that much."

I sat down. "So what now?"

"Kitty and I have been talking about it—"

"I just talked to the police again. They want to speak to everyone who knew you were at the Beverly Hillshire. Especially Sloan Baker."

"They're convinced it wasn't a simple robbery, dear," Kitty said. "They're going on the presumption that it all points to the manuscript."

"Well, that's brilliant. Whoever it was left forty bucks and my watch sitting on the table. Obviously he was after something else."

"Or she," said Elise.

Danziger made a face. "Thanks, Elise."

Elise drifted back into the kitchen, giving me a conspiratorial smile.

The pasta tasted as good as it smelled: light and fresh, herbed with flecks of fresh basil. I couldn't get it on my fork fast enough. I always preferred home cooking to restaurant food, as long as I wasn't the cook.

"So what exactly *was* stolen?" Danziger wanted to know.

"The only things missing, besides Sloan Baker and her wardrobe, were my laptop, the disks, Felina's original manuscript, and the one hard copy of the Felina book that was in the safe. Nothing else."

Kitty smiled. "The hotel's insurance will get you a new computer, dear."

"Pardon my French, but to hell with the computer." Danziger poured a glass of San Pellegrino. "Somebody has a copy of this manuscript."

"Manuscript . . ." My voice trickled away.

Jack stopped in mid-bite. "*What? What's wrong?*"

"There was another manuscript in that room," I said slowly. "I forgot to tell the police about it. I completely forgot I had it."

"Another copy?"

"Another *manuscript*, Jack. Vernon Ash's manuscript."

"Ash?"

"I interviewed him a few days ago."

"In jail?"

"He's out now. And he gave me the manuscript to a book he was writing. He wanted me to ghost it for him. That was taken, too."

"Vernon Ash?" Danziger looked interested. "What did he say in it?"

"Nothing. No great loss. It was pretty terrible," I added hastily. Christ, he was a regular deal-making pachinko machine.

"Sailors and ports?" said Danziger.

"What?"

"That's what you need in a tell-all. Which sailors, which ports. Names and dates. No one outside of L.A. remembers Vernon Ash. He'd have to get real specific—"

"Oh. No sailors. No ports."

"We could always spiff it up," said Kitty. "It might make an interesting follow-up to Felina's book. Would you be interested, dear?"

"I'd like to get this one done first," I said dryly. "And find a place to sleep tonight."

"The Beverly Hillshire wasn't a good idea to begin with. There's hundreds of employees there. Some of them have to be tabloid informants," said Kitty.

"There's only one place in town we could think of that the tabloids haven't been able to get into," added Jack. "Yet, at least."

"Where's that?" I asked, trying not to sound disappointed. There went my fantasy of sleeping in Jack's guest room, swimming in the pool, and eating Elise's cooking. I'd already pictured myself becoming the Youthful Ward of Danziger Manor.

"St. Elizabeth's."

My fork stopped halfway to my mouth.

= 14 =

JACK AND KITTY GRINNED at me, delighted at my response. "Come on," I said doubtfully. "You're kidding, right?"

"Why not?"

"For one, I'm not sick. Why would I stay in a hospital? And this isn't just a hospital. It's *St. Liz*."

St. Liz was a five-story marble cake located incongruously in a Santa Monica residential neighborhood. When it was built in the 1940s, it was known as St.-Elizabeth's-by-the-Sea, a place of none-too-fancy sickbeds for the folks of West L.A. Everyday people—at least the ones with good health insurance—still went there to get their prostates probed and their gallbladders removed. St. Liz also had formidable oncology and HIV wards, but that wasn't why the rich and famous flocked there for treatment from D.C. and Aspen and Biarritz.

St. Liz was the elective-surgery capital of Southern California, if not the world.

The doctors there were the leading authorities on rhinoplasties, blepharoplasties, dermabrasion, tummy tucks, cheek implants, and liposuction. They lifted faces, foreheads, eyelids, necks, and butts. They deadened facial nerves to reduce wrinkles and painted their patients' faces with trichloroacetic acid for a more dewy complexion. If you wanted an extra-slim waist-line, there was always the option of removing a few ribs. Some surgeons were even injecting botulin into their patients' faces to remove wrinkles. It also left them unable to form facial expressions, but what price beauty?

"I can't afford that, Kitty. I couldn't afford a bottle of aspirin at St. Elizabeth's."

"What if someone else picked up the tab?"

"Like who, Kitty?"

Kitty took a birdlike bite of pasta, looking smug. "The Beverly Hillshire can."

"What?"

"It was Kitty's idea," said Danziger. "I thought it was weird, too, but it makes sense. In a weird way."

"The hotel doesn't want it to get out that someone could get up to the thirty-fourth floor, much less get into a locked room, right? So I had Jack call his lawyer—"

"Gilbert called over to the hotel this morning and talked to the management. Made a little rumbling about lawsuits and publicity—"

"So they asked if we'd be willing to be compensated, aside from the material losses—"

"And Gilbert suggested that things might be averted if they'd foot the bill to put you up 'somewhere a little more secure.' And that's when he brought up St. Liz's."

"It's not a typical hospital room," soothed Kitty. "It's Four West. I've been up there. The rooms there are like little suites. Felina stayed there for a while. You'll be able to relax and not worry about anyone bothering you anymore."

"Safe as Air Force One," said Jack. "I know for a fact that

the tabloids haven't been able to get in there. And they've tried everything."

Once again, someone was planning my life for me.

"Do I really have to?"

"Sport, somebody's got your manuscript, Felina's manuscript, the tapes, everything," said Danziger. "If they sell 'em, we could probably sue, but it would still kill our project here. No one's gonna buy this book if they've already read it in the tabs or seen it on TV."

"I'm taking you over there at four o'clock." Kitty checked her watch. "You can get settled and get down to work immediately. You have to work fast, dear. Very fast. You don't have five days anymore."

"How long do I have?"

"Seventy-two hours."

We outfoxed the media—outfaxed them, actually.

Jack's assistant faxed a press release to the assignment desks, saying he would be having a press conference at four o'clock at Danziger Press. Right after lunch, he left for the office, telling the news crews outside that he'd answer all their questions at four. Two of the three vans packed up immediately and left. The *Headline Journal* crew hung around for a few more minutes, but by three o'clock they were gone, too.

When the street was clear, I put my car in Danziger's garage and climbed into Kitty's Mercedes. The door shut with an authoritative *thunk*, like a bank vault.

"Oh, I almost forgot," Kitty said, turning over the motor. "Look in the backseat."

It was a bag from Computer City. Inside was a brand-new laptop.

"I don't know beans about computers. Is it the right one?" she said, in the tone of a grandmother asking if the Christmas sweater fit.

"It's great." It was an IBM-compatible, not a Mac, but who cared? It was state-of-the-art, and my stolen PowerBook was the cyberequivalent of a '79 Pacer. "Thank you."

"You can thank the management of the Beverly Hillshire for that." Kitty backed out of the driveway, chuckling. "They seem to want to get on your good side."

We caught Wilshire going west. The beautiful day had held. The sky behind the buildings on Miracle Mile was delft-blue, and the palms lining the boulevard looked majestic instead of ratty. I hugged the new computer on my lap. Life was good, at least for the moment, and these days I was learning to savor those tiny instants.

Kitty drove like an old lady: leaning forward over the steering wheel, hands at ten and two o'clock, chattering away. "Hand me those sunglasses, dear, would you? Thank you. You can put on the radio if you like. Just no hard rock, please." She fumbled the glasses on. "This has been a heck of a day. Right after I drop you off, I'm going out to Century City to meet with this gal who called my office a few days ago. Seems she did a layout for *Playhouse*. Well, it turns out that she's studying at some Bible college back East and it's turned into a big hoo-hah. They're trying to expel her, but the girl's got some moxie."

I laughed. "Kitty, how did you get involved in all this?"

"All what, dear?"

"The scandal business."

"I've been around a long time. I'm a survivor." We stopped at a red light in front of the La Brea Tar Pits. "Do I have lipstick on my teeth, dear? Hand me that box of tissues."

"What did you do before you were a talent agent?"

"Well, I'm from Indiana. I came to Hollywood a long time ago, when I was very young. I'm almost as old as that fellow there," she said, pointing to a mastadon sculpture stuck in the tar. "But I could type sixty words a minute and I knew Gregg shorthand, so I figured I could get a job in the movie industry. I got an apartment in Carthay Circle and a job in the typing pool at Metro. There was one fellow there who kept requesting me. He was a press agent—we didn't have the term 'publicist' back then. And his name was Harry Keyes. Harry asked me to marry him, and we went independent and set up our own shop. Keyes and Keyes. Harry taught me how to be a press agent."

"Those days always sound like more fun," I said wistfully.

"Well, they were. You would have enjoyed it. This town was like a big club where everyone knew one another. The war was over. Times were good. People had money and style and fun."

A fragrance ad went past on the right. The usual emaciated jailbait model stared out of a grainy black-and-white billboard. Who the hell would want to smell like her?

"What kind of publicity did you do?"

"Silly things. Stunts, really. We would take some starlet and cook up an award for her. Make a big deal out of it. 'The West Coast Milliners' Guild gave its prestigious Chapeau Award to so-and-so.' We'd rent some crazy hats from Western Costume, take a few pictures of the girl, and send them out all over the country. Of course, no one knew that the West Coast Milliners' Guild was me and Harry." She laughed.

"So how did you switch from press agent to talent agent?"

"Harry died in the Sixties. After that, it wasn't any fun." She nosed the Mercedes through a yellow light at Robertson. "Not just because he was gone, but the whole business seemed to change. No one dressed up and went out at night anymore. The nightclubs closed. All anyone could think about was Vietnam. And we didn't have movie stars anymore, we had *actors*. Dustin Hoffman, Jane Fonda . . .

"So I gathered up some of the old-timers who weren't working and tried to find them jobs. It worked, for a while, but then most of them died off or retired. The only new clients I ever had were people who'd been dropped by every other agency in town."

"You really enjoy this, don't you?"

"My dear, I love it. At my age, who would have guessed that this old broad would still be working? And something about it feels like the old days. A lot of nonsense and razzamatazz."

Kitty chuckled. "In a way, Scandal Inc. was the biggest publicity stunt I ever pulled."

My clothes were still at the Beverly Hillshire, so I had Kitty stop at Claudia's so I could pick up a few things. Fortunately, Claudia's car was gone. I wasn't up to dealing with her. Or Lydia and the other Dubuissons, for that matter.

"I'll just wait out here, dear. You take your time," said Kitty. Translation: Make it snappy.

The place was more of a mess than ever, with Lydia's suitcases open atop my packing boxes. Her presence was everywhere: gardenia scent, a scarlet blouse draped over a chair, gaudy earrings in the ceramic bowl where I kept my keys, next to a Hot Wheels track. A stack of true-crime paperbacks and airport novels—the kind of stuff Claudia never read—sat on the computer station. My laundry was stacked in a corner of the living room, just where I'd left it the night before Shelly Nguyen knocked on the door and my life spun out of control.

I slipped on the outfit I liked to wear at the computer: a T-shirt, my old high-top Converses, and a pair of black gym shorts with RHODES on the rear. Going to the hospital, okay, but I was damned if I was going to write *Mann's Woman* while wearing a papery gown that gave the world a view of my ass.

My shaving kit was in the trunk at the foot of Claudia's bed. Back when we had separate apartments, I kept a second set of toiletries at her place: razor, shaving gel, toothbrush, lens case, a tube of Speed Stick. There were also a couple of condoms at the bottom, along with a tiny tube of nonoxynol-9 lubricant. We hadn't had to use those for a while. In fact, I couldn't remember the last time we'd made love.

The place didn't feel like home anymore.

I put the shaving kit and several changes of clothes into a spare suitcase and started to write a note on the telephone pad, but I couldn't think of anything to say past *Claude*.

I wadded it up and threw it in the trash.

On the way out the door, I realized that I didn't have anything to read. The nearest thing was Lydia's stack of books, and I wasn't up for true crime these days. At the bottom was a novel with an embossed-foil cover, the kind of thing you'd buy at an airport concession and leave in the seat pocket when you deplaned. *77 Rodeo Drive*, it was called. Jocelyn had a whole stable of writers cranking out these things, which she called "shop-and-fucks."

What the heck, I thought, throwing it into my suitcase. After all, I was on my way to the very heart of shop-and-fuck.

"There's the parking entrance," I said as we cruised by the famous fountain in front.

"That's not what we're looking for, dear."

Kitty drove down a side street and made an abrupt left turn into an unmarked driveway that slanted down. At the foot of the drive was a guard shack and a gate—not a striped-arm wooden gate, but a rolling steel portcullis that looked like it could repel a camisado by Leo Lazarnick's Darth Vader van.

The guard went around to the back of the Mercedes and checked the license plate before approaching the driver's window.

"Welcome to St. Elizabeth's," he said. "Pop the trunk for me, please. While I check that, you can get out your identification."

Satisfied that there weren't any *Celeb* reporters hiding in the trunk, the guard took our driver's licenses and murmured into a phone. The gate rolled open, and we drove down another level to a small parking garage. There was an elevator door there, framed with ficuses. A woman in a blue business suit was waiting.

"Kieran O'Connor? Hi, I'm Linda Jackson. I'll be helping you get settled." She smiled at Kitty. "I'm sorry, ma'am, but from this point on it's patients only."

"Thanks, Kitty. I really appreciate it."

"All in a day's work. It was a cinch. You'll call me and let me know how it's going?"

"Of course. Bye, Kitty."

"Good-bye, dear." She gave me a rosewater-scented kiss.

I watched her drive back up the ramp, feeling a little pang of sadness. If Kitty Keyes was forty years younger, I might have asked her out.

I don't know what I expected from St. Liz's—Armani hospital gowns, gold-plated bedpans, and IV bottles made of Steuben glass—but 4 West felt like a spa. The hall was extra-wide, to accommodate gurneys and such, but the floor was carpeted, and the halls were softly lit by hidden wall sconces. Vivaldi played from unseen speakers. Hockney swimming-pool prints hung on the walls. That familiar hospital scent—medicine, disinfectant, and the unmistakable smell of sickness—was replaced by a light whiff of jasmine.

And then I passed a woman in a wheelchair. Her face was bright red and blotchy, with dots of blood seeping out around the bandages, and surgical tape crosses were stretched across her nose. She looked like the victim of an acid-throwing attack.

"How are you doing today, Mrs. Young?" Linda asked.

"Mmfnn," Mrs. Young said. The effort made a fresh flower of blood bloom under her bandages, and my lunch lurched in my stomach.

Linda took me into a sitting room and filled out my check-in information. "Sign this," she told me. "I know it's complicated, but read it all. We have to sign 'em, too."

AGREEMENT OF CONFIDENTIALITY, it said at the top. The

rules had been written in English, but this jobbie was in pure lawyerese. All the *whereases* and *heretofores* added up to just one thing: If I ("hereafter known as the 'Patient' ") ever breathed a word about anything or anyone I saw at St. Elizabeth's ("hereafter known as the 'Health Care Facility' "), my ass would be grass and the St. Liz legal team would have my spleen for breakfast.

"Do you get approached by the press a lot?"

"I can't tell you that. But when it does happen, we're required to report it to our supervisors immediately. If we don't, that's grounds for termination. We're very serious about protecting our patients here."

Linda took my picture with a device that looked like the driver's license machine at the DMV. The I.D. the machine spit out was a white plastic card that hung around my neck by a cloth ribbon. On the back was a magnetic strip. The front said O'CONNOR KIERAN. "Keep that on," she said. "If you have to leave the floor, you'll need it to get back."

Rumor had it that the rooms on 4 West were like suites at the Beverly Hillshire. Not quite, but not bad. The bed had a cherry headboard, the carpet was Berber, and the TV stood in a mahogany armoire instead of hanging from a ceiling bracket. Floor-length drapes covered the facing wall. A small desk/dining table combo was tucked into one corner. But there were handrails on the walls, and a nurses' station call button draped over the headboard.

"You'll find outlets and such for your computer behind the table," Linda told me. "There's a copy of the meal plan on the nightstand. Make your selection and leave it on the door by the time specified. If you want something that's not on the menu, or if you just get hungry, there's a call button on the phone for our chef."

"Chef?"

"Four West has its own chef. You don't have any dietary restrictions, so you can have whatever you want." Linda stopped at the door. "If you need anything, just call Veronica in Guest Services. That button's on your phone, too."

I laughed. "This hospital has a concierge?"

"Welcome to St. Elizabeth's," she said, smiling, and closed the door behind her.

It shut with a soft, authoritative *click*.

Well, I thought, how can I get the Beverly Hillshire to pay for this for the rest of my life?

I turned on the radio, which was preset to a New Age station, and unpacked what few clothes I'd brought into the lowboy. All set. The drapes were on the south-facing wall. Maybe I could catch the last of the afternoon sun.

I drew them and was surprised to find more wallpaper. No window at all.

St. Liz was serious about security.

Just try to get me now, Brooks Levin.

I unpacked my computer from its bubble-wrap swaddling and began looking over the manual, but there was an uneasiness I hadn't felt before.

I felt as though I'd landed in a velvet-lined safe-deposit box.

15

I SPENT THE EVENING unpacking the computer, reading the manual, and noodling with some of the features. By nine o'clock, I was already nodding off, so I climbed into bed and got my first good night's sleep in days.

4B12 turned out to be the ideal writing environment. With no windows and the clock turned to the wall, the room felt hermetically sealed, like a bathysphere or a casino. Meals showed up without me asking. The only reading material in the room was my shop-and-fuck, which I didn't even crack.

Using the information I'd gleaned from Leo Lazarnick, Betty Bradford Mann, and Sloan Baker, I padded out the extant manuscript, filling in blanks, guessing at motivations, reconstructing scenes and conversations. Instead of fussing over every sentence, I wrote in a straight line, never looking back. When the pain in my spine became too intense to ignore, I walked the halls, chatted with the duty nurses, read magazines in the lounge, and played Minesweeper on my new computer. But I kept going back, and by the time I went to bed, I'd written sixty-three pages.

In the old movies, they'd type "-30-." I settled for "The End."

Were there any more beautiful words in the English language?

THE END. One hundred eighty-four pages of double-spaced, spell-checked bull. I saved the floppy I'd been working on to the hard drive and made a couple more floppy copies. Danziger and Jocelyn could each have one. So could Brooks Levin, for that matter.

Jack Danziger was at his desk when I called. "It's done."

"Way to go, Sport. When can I see it?"

"Whenever you want. I don't have a printer with me, so it's still on a floppy."

"I can have my secretary print it out." Papers rustled. "I'm coming to the Westside tonight for a dinner thing. Can I swing by and get it on the way back?"

"Sure. I thought I'd stay one more night and check out of here tomorrow morning."

"You're a champ. Hey, I've got a surprise for you when I get there," he said, and hung up.

I rolled my neck and checked the clock. Four in the afternoon, and one day ahead of schedule. Not bad, even if the book itself was crap.

I lay down and did my back stretches. It didn't help. I couldn't close off my mind as easily as I could a computer file. My left brain and my right brain just kept niggling.

The book might have been done, but there was one thing those two sides of my brain agreed on: Something was wrong with this story.

Mann's Woman might be just fine for the mouth-breathers who bought *Celeb* and watched *Headline Journal*. It had sex; it had death; it had Hollywood.

But there was certainly nothing worthy of Brooks Levin's interest, much less worthy of breaking into a hotel room and cracking a safe to discover.

Was there?

Not that I'd found. But something felt incomplete. There was something in the center of the Felina Lopez story like a black hole. Everything seemed to revolve around it, but I just couldn't see it. There was nothing in that manuscript worth stealing.

But maybe someone didn't know that, O'Connor.

I wasn't going to be able to rest until I knew what it was.

"Sally Comiskey."

"Hey, Sal. It's Kieran."

"On deadline." Her keyboard hadn't stopped clicking. "What do you need?"

"Can you have the library pull some clips for me?"

"On deadline, Kieran. You remember what that means?"

"It's important."

"Life or death?"

"No . . ."

"This is. Call back tomorrow. After ten," she said, and hung up.

Thanks, Sal.

Now what?

My computer bleeped. A screen saver came on. Trapezoids, folding and unfolding in space.

There was one other person I could call to get the information I needed. The question was: How bad did I want to know?

I stared at the trapezoids unfolding. It was a beautiful laptop, all tricked out with a CD-ROM player and an internal modem for sending E-mail and surfing the Internet.

I sat up.

If the computer only had the software built in . . .

It did.

Ten minutes later I was on the Internet, accessing the alt.truecrime newsgroup that Lydia had told me about. It was a long shot, but most of a reporter's job is just fishing in empty holes.

Most of the postings were about other cases. Apparently interest in the case had waned. Still, there were a few with FELINA in the subject title. I chose one at random.

>I think Felina was kiled because she knew something. Shehad traveled in circles where she would learn alotof secrets. Maybe one of the men she slept with thought she was going to write about his business dealings, maybe one of them was maried. Anyway, I think it was MURDER and not some acidental robbery thing. What was in that book that was so dangerous that is what I would like to know . . .

Yeah. Me, too. I clicked to the next message.

>This whole thing points to one person: Vernon Ash. She sent him to jail. He's out now and ready to even the score.

The theory was a little too pat, but maybe Ash thought her book would somehow have the same information as his. People killed for less every day.

>>Homicide investigators look at one thing: motive. In this case I think it's safe to say that the motive is profit—not necessarily financial profit, but profit nonetheless. The cops ought to be asking themselves: who stands to profit from Felina Lopez's death?

Me, for one. Danziger and Kitty Keyes, for two and three. And Jocelyn, for that matter. But I couldn't think of anyone else. Betty Mann? No, the Dick/Felina stuff had already been covered ad extreme nauseum in the tabs and on television. Ash? His life story was public record; besides, he was ready to talk about it to anyone who would listen.

I clicked through the other postings rapidly.

>>Sounds like a drug deal to me.

>>Maybe she was still turning tricks. Maybe she was into kinky sex (S and M) and one of her customers went too far. Maybe that's what happened.

>>This is all a big publecity stunt, the crime scene was obviously STAGED so her book would do well, Falina is "LAUGHING ALL THE WAY TOO THE BANK" and living somehwere probably in MEXICO. She will split the $$$ with her publisher when it becomes a bestsleler, I wont buy it because it is WORNG to be a whore.

»Did Felina's "little black book" ever come to light? Would love to know who was in it . . .

»Was Felina a lesbian? She sure looked like a dyke to me. And I'd like the chance to set her "straight" ‹ha ha›

»I think Betty Bradford Mann found out what she was doing with her husband and "O.J.'d" Felina! ;-)

»Does everything *have* to be a conspiracy theory? Can't this just be a rich lady who got offed in a robbery gone wrong? Haven't you people ever heard of Occam's razor?

»All I know is: this is gonna sell a hell of a lot more books than it would if she were alive.

If there were any words of wisdom there, I couldn't see them.

I had one option left.

Sighing, I picked up the phone again and dialed.

"*Celeb*," said a voice with a Texas twang.

"Gina Guglielmelli, please. This is Kieran O'Connor, returning her call." She hadn't called me, of course, but I always used the line to get past receptionist roadblocks.

Miss Texas sent me into the hold ether, where I got to hear an elevator version of "Smells Like Teen Spirit" before a speakerphone picked up.

"Guglielmelli."

"It's Kieran O'Connor."

"O'Connor. O. *Connor.*" She was enjoying this. I pictured her leaning back in her chair, folding her arms behind her head.

"Can you take me off speaker, please?"

She picked up. "What do you need, O'Connor?"

"Information."

"Dial four-one-one."

"Just tell me how much I'm gonna have to grovel so I can get started, okay?"

A laugh. "What do you need?"

"What do you know about Brooks Levin?"

When she spoke, her voice was guarded. "He's a P.I. and a personal-security expert. If you want to know if he's worked for *Celeb,* I don't know anything about that."

"That's not what I . . ."

I sighed. This felt like the end of the road—telling a tab reporter that I was being pursued by Brooks Levin. Unfortunately, she was the only one who could help me.

"O'Connor? Is something wrong?" Her voice had a note of genuine concern. Or else she was a damn good actress.

I weighed how much to tell Gina Guglielmelli, and then I told her everything.

"You're sure he's the one who broke into your hotel?"

"I don't have proof. But who else could it have been? Sloan Baker couldn't pick her nose, much less a safe."

"And you don't have any idea who he could be working for? Because, believe me, it's not us."

"I don't." I paused. "Gina, if this was you, would you feel like you were in any danger?"

"No. Not now, at least. Think about it. Getting that manuscript stolen was the best thing that ever happened to you."

"Why?"

"Somebody wanted to see what you were going to write. Assume Levin or his client—or clients—have read it. You said yourself there were no major revelations in there. So you've got nothing to worry about, right?"

"But . . . if someone's that interested, there must be more to the story than I've been able to find out."

"O'Connor . . ." She sighed. "I'll deny I ever told you this. But I've been ahead of you on this from jump street, and I can assure you there's just nothing more out there. I'm sure the only thing you've got that I don't is Felina's manuscript. And you've already told me there's nothing explosive in there."

"There isn't. But I'm sure there's something else."

"Assuming that's true—and I don't believe it, by the way— is it worth sticking your neck on the chopper to find out what it might be? This isn't Watergate."

"I guess not . . ."

"Look, O'Connor. I don't know Brooks Levin, but I've heard the same things you have. He's a strong-arm and a bully. But he doesn't come after people with guns. He wins through intimidation. You haven't heard anything from him since your manuscript was stolen, have you? So get it out on the stands, toot sweet. And then move on to your next project ASAP. Now get off my phone. I've got work to do."

"Thanks, Gina. I owe you dinner, I guess. Or something."

"Don't sweat it."

"No, I owe you a favor."

"Oh, I know you do. A big one. Don't you forget that." She

laughed. "You watch your back, O'Connor. I want to be able to collect."

I hung up, feeling moody and broody and thoughtful. The room felt like a four-star jail cell. I needed a break.

Down in the 4 West lounge, a picture window gave me a perfect view of the city and the Santa Monica Bay. Shadows were getting long in the yard, and the sun hung over the Pacific like a blood orange.

The only other person there was a leathery, sixtyish man who wore tinted sunglasses and a chestnut toupee of some space-age material. My guess was Ban-Lon. He was reading a copy of *Biz*. There was a tumbler of melted ice and Coke on the table next to him, two inches away from a coaster. The glass was sweating its way into the wood, making a chalky ring.

He peered at me through the sunglasses. "Hey, hey, I'm Sid McKay."

"Kieran O'Connor." We shook hands. There was a plum-colored half moon under each of his eyes. An eyebag-ectomy.

"Sit down, sit down," he said. "You want a drink? The nurse is on his way back with another one for me."

"I'm fine."

"Come on. You're not one of those mineral-water types, are ya?" Sid guffawed. "Kids today, they act like having a drink or eating a steak is like taking freakin' arsenic."

"Maybe I'll get some juice or something."

"Juice. Horse manure. Live a little, live a little. C'mon, isn't this place great?" Sid leaned back expansively and shifted his weight in the chair with a groan. There was some sort of special rubber pillow under his butt. "I been to most of 'em. Wilson Pavilion at UCLA, the eighth floor at Cedars, but St. Elizabeth's is the way to go. This is like a vacation."

"Working vacation for me."

One of the Armani nurses came in with a fresh glass on a tray. "Cuba Libre, Sid."

"Bring this young Irishman one, too." The nurse/waiter smiled and slipped out. "Working vacation. What, you working on a screenplay or something?"

"Something like that."

"Thought so. You look like a writer." Sid grinned. "I'm in indie prod myself."

"Indie prod" was independent film production. Some independent producers actually had studio deals, but generally indie prod was the glue factory for has-been studio execs and terminal wannabes.

"What kind of stuff do you do, Sid?"

"Mostly foreign distribution. I do a lot of business out at the festivals. Cannes, Berlin, Toronto, you know?"

"Oh, yeah, I know." There were some good independent pictures at the festivals, but most of it was straight-to-video dreck with tits for days and self-consciously campy titles like *Space Sluts Invade Uranus*.

My Cuba Libre arrived. The rum was coconut-flavored and smelled like sunblock. Tasted like it, too, but I drank half of it in one swallow.

"Christ, my ass hurts," Sid announced, pulling the pillow from under his posterior and plumping it up.

"Hemorrhoids, Sid?"

"Nah. Lipo. Hemorrhoids I ain't got." He knocked the table next to him. "Hey, you know what they did with the fat they sucked out of there?"

"Uh-uh."

He pointed at his lap.

"I don't get it."

Sid leaned over, grimacing from the pain. "My dick," he said. "They took it out of my ass and put it in my dick. A penis extension."

"They put the fat cells from your butt into your—"

"Actually, *extension* isn't really the right word. It's more a width thing than a length thing, if you get my driftarooney." Sid beamed. "My M.D. says I'll be hung like a beer can."

I was thirty pages into my shop-and-fuck when Jack rang up. "They won't let me up to Four West. I'm in the visitors' lounge on three."

"On my way," I said. The guard at the 4 West elevator sent me back to my room to pick up my I.D. badge. St. Liz was serious about security.

The lounge felt like a fish tank: all dim lights and glass. A digital clock on the table said 9:32 P.M. in iridescent green numerals.

Jack Danziger was staring out the window, wearing one of his silk-armored power suits. Outside, the lights of Santa Monica glimmered in the purple-black. A fat moon had replaced the sun, hanging over the bay, shimmering like mercury in the dark water. If I cared to look, I could probably pick out Fourteenth Street and Claudia's neighborhood. I didn't care to look.

"Hey, Jack."

He turned around and grinned. "K-man. So how do you like this boot camp?"

"It's great."

"Told you. It's just like a hotel."

I handed him the disk. "What brings you down here?"

"I had a dinner thing on the Promenade with another one of Kitty's clients. She's got some doozies." He shook his head.

"You're doing another book?"

"I don't know yet. This was more a meet-and-greet."

"What's it about?"

"I could tell ya, but then I'd have to kill ya." He laughed. "But forget that. I told you I had a surprise for you. The cops called me this afternoon. Your buddy Sloan turned up."

"Alive?"

Danziger looked nonplussed. "Of course alive. What made you . . ."

"Nothing, nothing. So what happened? The police picked her up?"

"No, they found her car in a lot at LAX and did a trace of the airline schedules. She'd flown up to San Francisco with some rich john. Get this: From what the cop told me, she'd met the dude while she was staying in your suite at the Hillshire. He was staying at the hotel for business and going on to San Francisco. Some import/export guy based in Central America. He'd paid her fare to SFO and tucked her into a room at the Mark Hopkins. She's coming back tonight for a little chat with the BHPD." He clapped his hands. "The last piece of the puzzle comes together, eh? And we got our book and your computer back."

"She had the manuscript on her? And the computer?"

"They didn't say that. But who else would have done it?"

"No one, I guess."

Neither of us said anything for a minute.

"Well. Anyway. I've got one of my assistants lining up the photo permissions. Wish there was someone we could tap to write a forword, but I don't see it happening on this one."

"Well, I wouldn't ask Betty Bradford Mann," I mumbled.

"You're funny," Danziger said absently, but he wasn't really listening. He walked back toward the window. "Big old moon tonight, huh?"

"Big old moon."

He stuck one paw into his pocket. It disappeared in folds of silk. Change jingled.

"So are you happy with the way it turned out?"

"That's for you to say, Jack."

"Sure, but are you?"

"It's what you want."

"It sounds like there's a *but* at the end of that sentence, Sport."

I stared out the window at his big old moon. Danziger was looking at me strangely. "I just can't figure out what's so hot in this that someone would try to steal it," I said.

"Nothing. But they don't know that." He shrugged. "These tabloid characters, they didn't know what we had. That's why they wanted to get their hands on it. They were the ones who played up how hot it was, and they finally started to believe their own bullshit. Self-fulfilling prophecy." He laughed again. "What are we supposed to do? Correct 'em?"

Behind him, far away, a plane took off over the Pacific: two blinking red lights and one white.

I couldn't sleep. I played Minesweeper, sent an E-mail to Jeff Brenner, and watched TV. At one-thirty, I was too tired to sleep.

The black hole was still out there. Now that I didn't have the pressure of the deadline, it was all I could think about. So what if it wasn't done? So what if it wasn't complete?

Jocelyn Cricket whispered in my ear again: *Good isn't the point. Done is.*

Jocelyn was right. *Good* sold a couple thousand copies, brought a trickle of people into the theater, made a few critics happy, and got the back of the hand from the rest of the world. And good—as in honor and virtue—didn't matter, either. Once, the world had revered astronauts and artists, inventors and innovators. Then the Zeitgeist had some fundamental shift, and we were looking up to athletes and actors. Even that seemed like a long time ago now.

Today we were in a new world where fame itself was its own commodity: fame without achievement, be it grand or base. Fame its ownself. Jocelyn and Kitty repped it, Jack Danziger marketed it, and the whole nation bought it. Dick Mann and Felina Lopez and Vernon Ash and even Leo Lazarnick—all of them were tissue-thin, personae with neither style nor substance, just names that had been whirled in the pop-culture blender and served up like an eight-dollar protein shake at Smooth Moo.

And when *Mann's Woman* was published, one more name would be added to that list: mine.

If I wasn't so tired, if my back wasn't in spasm, I might have cared. Instead, it just seemed like cheap philosophy.

The windowless room was making me claustrophobic again. I picked up my shop-and-fuck and went down the hall to the lounge, where I sat down in Sid McKay's chair and looked out over the lights of the city. No one was around; our rum-and-Coke glasses were still sitting there, each with a lime slice at the bottom like a drowned mouse.

An embryo of an idea began to grow in my mind.

The drink . . .

. . . Sid McKay . . .

. . . something Sid had said . . .

. . . reminded me of something Felina once said . . .

. . . which might be important.

Might be, I reminded myself. But Felina had given me one clue that had gone right over my head, a clue that might be worth following up. It might add up to nothing, but it was worth a few phone calls in the morning.

I sat in the lounge for an hour, wondering where I'd go when I checked out in the morning, wondering where I'd live. Brenner would let me stay for a while, I was sure, but what next? And what next for Claudia and me?

After a while, I padded back to my room, switched off the light, and climbed into bed. It was a quarter to three by now, and my body craved sleep, but the two halves of my brain were clicking now, and the sprig of thought just wouldn't stop growing, working in my head like sand in an oyster.

= 16 =

GUEST SERVICES SENT UP the L.A. phone directories—both White and Yellow Pages—along with my morning coffee. Why do people waste so much money on J-school, I wondered, when ninety percent of a reporter's job is just talking on the phone?

There were more listings than I'd thought, most of them in downtown L.A. Nothing to do but take them in alphabetical order.

The man who answered the phone at the first number spoke only Spanish. The second couldn't help me. Neither could the third, or the fourth, or the fifth.

The sixth number was answered by a woman. Young, too, from the sound of her.

"This is Marga Garza."

"Hi, Ms. Garza. I was looking for—"

"We're not open," she interrupted. "I'm just the book-keeper. If you want to place an order, call back after ten, okay?"

"Maybe you can help me. I'm looking for Eduardo Lopez."

"Lopez?" she said, sounding puzzled.

"Right. He'd be in his sixties or seventies. I was thinking there might be someone there who knew him—"

"*Knew* him?" She paused. "He just got here a few minutes ago. You want to talk to him? Hang on."

She put her hand over the receiver and yelled at someone to get Eduardo.

I hung up.

I still didn't know what the black hole at the middle of Felina's story was, but I had one last chance to find out.

Leaving St. Liz was easy. I didn't even bother to check out; I just picked up my laptop, put my floppies inside, and left.

Once I was through the lobby and out the front door, it was a two-block walk up Twenty-third Street to Wilshire and the bus shelter. I was safe, I kept telling myself. If Brooks Levin was still interested in me, he would have already found out where I was staying.

What he *wouldn't* be expecting was that I would leave my hidey-hole and take a city bus.

Waiting for the eastbound RTD, I sighed. Once, I would have called Claudia for a ride and asked her to tag along. If my lead panned out, we might even have gone for lunch afterward: sushi in Little Tokyo, brisket at the Pantry . . .

The bus pulled up, cutting my reverie short.

I was on my own this time.

I left the bus at Rossmore and walked the few blocks over to Danziger's place. Not a soul was on the streets of Hancock Park. A Southtec car came by, slowing down as it passed me. Angelenos might be fanatical about walking when it comes to treadmills, but on the streets of L.A., pedestrians are automatically suspicious characters.

Elise opened the kitchen door. Behind her, a broomstick had been laid across two chairs. It was hung with freshly made pasta, drying like laundry on a clothesline.

"Hey, you," she said, wiping her floury hands on her apron. "Jack's not here. Were you supposed to meet him?"

"Nah. Just came to pick up my car."

"It's still in the garage. In *my* space, I might add. Hey, why don't you stay and eat lunch with me? I'm making pasta *puttanesca*."

"What's that?"

"Tomato sauce with olives and anchovies. The literal translation is 'whore's spaghetti.'" She grinned. "It tastes better than it sounds."

"Sounds tempting, but I've got to run."

Backing out of the garage, I grinned.

Whore's spaghetti. Just what I'd been working on for the last few weeks.

I skirted the edge of Koreatown and drove through MacArthur Park. Once one of the most beautiful parks in the city, it was now an open-air, twenty-four-hour drug supermarket. *Someone left my crack out in the rain . . .*

From MacArthur Park it was a locked-door drive through the dangerous Pico-Union neighborhood, a quick sprint under the 110, and then I was on Sixth Street, headed into downtown L.A.

In the Eighties, the city had built some glitzy loft-condos down here, trying to lure rich yuppies back to the heart of the city, but the effort had failed and many of the lofts sat empty. All the Jacuzzis and industrial-gray carpeting in the world can't make up for junkies bobbing and weaving on your stoop.

Past the skyscrapers and the glass box office towers was the real downtown, a seedy district of fruit and flower warehouses, flophouse hotels, and bars where a toothpaste-sized glass of Schlitz was still a quarter. I passed one street lined with people sleeping in refrigerator boxes. In the winter, there were illegal bonfires, homeless families cuddling next to dogs for warmth, people stabbing one another to death over a blanket or a bag of aluminum cans. The address I was looking for was near Fifth and San Pedro, just down from the Double Nickel, an area so tough they hadn't even tried to redevelop it. I parked in a bulldozed lot that had been turned into a U-Park and pushed a five-dollar bill through a slot in a lockbox.

Walking down San Pedro, I missed it the first time. On my second pass-by, I found a small storefront with dirty windows, hidden by heavy metal gates. Faded white letters on the door spelled out the legend LUZ DEL MUNDO • FINE CIGARS • SINCE 1911 • TOTALAMENTE A MANO.

It was Sid McKay's rum-and-Coke that had given me the clue. Rum-and-Coke. Cuba Libre.

Because she'd lived in Puesta del Sol, I had assumed that Felina was Mexican herself. But she had told me at the Gallo Rojo that her father was a cigar roller. They made cigars in Mexico, too, of course, but Felina smoked Cubans. And there were only a few places in the city where a Cuban cigar roller could find work.

The door was locked. Damn. I tried the knob again, and this time the door buzzed and swung open.

Luz del Mundo could have been an ancient dry cleaners, with its high sloping counter and old-fashioned cash register. What hit me first, though, was the smell: cedar, damp earth, and the intoxicating odor of rich tobacco. The aroma was divine, as basic and satisfying as freshly baked bread. And under it all was another smell: musty air and history and the sweat of a hundred anonymous artisans. Overhead, a ceiling fan made lazy circles. A fat woman with a black bun and cakey lipstick sat at a high stool behind the counter, giving me the fish-eye.

I'd been to a few events at the "cigar bars" in Beverly Hills and had been turned off by their pretension and self-importance. Industry types spent thousands of dollars for the privilege of smoking their stogies there and renting a few cubic feet of air to store them in. But what nauseated me the most was the members, who seemed to think a twenty-five-dollar cigar transformed them from overpaid numbnuts into bad-boy rebels.

Those places sold status. Luz del Mundo sold cigars.

"Buenas dias," I said to the woman behind the counter.

"Buenas tardes."

She didn't take her dark eyes off me for a second. Something told me that (a) she didn't speak English and (b) she didn't like me too much. Asking for Eduardo would have been stupid. At the least, I would have gotten a *"No comprende."* More likely, I'd be out on my ass.

While I planned my next move, I examined the open boxes of cigars on display. They were formal and elegant. LUZ DEL MUNDO, they said in crimson letters. On the lids was an old-fashioned logo: a rising yellow sun and, in silhouette, a red rooster.

A red rooster.

El Gallo Rojo.

I was born in the Year of the Rooster . . . It's always an important year.

I fingered a couple of the cigars. They were dark and roughly finished, with a rich loamy smell that managed to combine new leather with antiquated dignity. Gold and red cigar bands duplicated the rooster/sun image from the boxes. There were four different sizes, all with bird names. The small panatelas were Gorriónes—sparrows—and the robustos, Halcónes—falcons. Then there were some strange triangular cigars, small at the tip and wide at the base. Torpedos, I remembered, from my trip to the Beverly Hills cigar bar. These were called Pavónes. Of course; peacocks.

The cigars in the fourth box were Churchill-sized, eight inches long and fat as a chunk of pipe. I picked one up to give it a sniff, and then I saw the name on the box:

Águilas.

La águila. A symbol of strength, fierceness, protection.

The eagle is a symbol. My familiar.

"Concepción?"

A woman came out of the back. She was about thirty-five, with curly brown hair, bright-yellow dangle earrings shaped like lemon slices, and zaftig hips. She rattled off something in Spanish to the woman at the register, who handed her a ledger book, never taking her eyes off me. Apparently I was a security risk.

"Marga?" I asked.

She looked at me, surprised. "Yeah?"

"Can I talk to you for a few minutes?"

"I don't know," she said agreeably. "Who are you?"

"My name's Kieran O'Connor. Is there somewhere else we can talk?"

Marga looked puzzled, but her curiosity was roused. "Sure. Come on back to my office."

I followed her behind the counter, the old woman shooting me a hooded look.

Marga Garza led me through a door that opened onto a large room redolent of tobacco. The gallery was warm as a greenhouse, lit with fluorescent fixtures that were harsh on the shabby ochre walls and peeling paint. If the scent of tobacco was intoxicating in the anteroom, here it was overpowering in its richness.

A couple dozen men and a few women, most of them old, sat at wooden desks, rolling sheaves of tobacco leaves into neat cylinders, with the same casual precision Elise used to chop her bell pepper. The men wore ribbed white tank tops and jeans; the women, cheap blouses. An unseen radio warbled sad *canciónes*. We could have been in Havana in the 1930s.

"Marga!" A man in a clip-on tie flagged her down. "You got those invoice numbers?"

She rolled her eyes at me. "Hang on a second."

The old man nearest me grabbed a handful of leaves and gave them a quick roll between his palms. Magically, the loose leaves turned into a crude cylinder. He picked up an odd knife-like object—a flat metal semicircle with a convex cutting edge—and gave the sticking-out leaves a whack. A few more twists in his palms, and it began to take the shape of a cigar. He used the flat part of his knife like a rolling pin to finish the sides and trimmed the straggly end. When he was done, he placed the cigar in a wooden mold where several other cigars were resting. I was fascinated.

"Yadda yadda yadda. What a pain in the butt." Marga was back, fumbling with a key in an office door. "C'mon in. There's not much room, but there's a folding chair behind you there."

It looked like a mop closet that had been converted into an office; my head brushed the ceiling. A small desk had been wedged under the stairs, next to an old wooden file cabinet with brass pulls. Ledgers, files, and Pendaflex folders were piled in liquor cartons, stacked everywhere. A battered ten-key spit out a paper tongue of figures that curled on the floor. Taped to the wall was a large sign that said NO SMOKING.

"Is this your family's business?" I asked.

Marga's eyes widened. "God, no. I mean, no. I used to do the books for a record company in San Diego. My husband moved us up here last year and then walked out on me a few months ago, the bastard. This is just transitional. At least I hope it is. They don't even have computers here. And they don't like me."

I grinned. "Why?"

"Oh, most of 'em are old-school Catholics. I made the mistake my first day of telling someone that I thought the Pope was a misogynist pig, and by lunch they were all acting like I was Rosemary's baby, getting all Hispanicker-than-thou with me. I grew up in a tract house in Wisconsin, not some apartment in the *barrio*. So sue me. Anyway." She puffed out her cheeks and blew air. "What did you want?"

"I called you earlier. About Eduardo Lopez."

Distrust began to make little furrows around her eyes. "What about him?"

"His daughter is dead. I came to tell him."

Marga looked blank. "His daughter?"

"I'm a reporter. I was ghost-writing a book with her. She was murdered a couple of weeks ago."

"His *daughter*? Sugar, are you sure? I think you might have the wrong Mr. Lopez."

"Her name was Felina. She was about forty."

Marga shook her head. "Hm-mm. No way. I eat lunch with Mr. Lopez sometimes. He would have mentioned a daughter."

"Are you sure?"

"Yes. I even go over to his house once in a while. He needs help going through his bills, writing checks. We usually end up having dinner. He would have mentioned a daughter by now. There's no pictures in that house. Nothing."

I sat back in the rickety folding chair, baffled. Lopez was a common name; Eduardo less so. But how many Eduardo Lopezes were working as cigar rollers in Los Angeles?

"Would you recognize his signature if you saw it?"

"I think so."

I handed her the model release I'd stolen from Leo Lazarnick. Marga looked at it for a long moment.

"That's strange," she said. "It looks . . . Hmm." She opened the file cabinet and pulled out a manila folder. "Here's Mr. Lopez's file. Look at this withholding form. I think it's a different person."

It was an old man's signature: shaky, cursive letters, slightly formal and antique. Not too close to the one on Lazarnick's model release, but the longer I looked, the more similarities I saw.

"Marga, look at the flourish on the capital E, and the L."

"Maybe," she said dubiously. "Mr. Lopez can't read. He can't write much more than his own name."

"This piece of paper I've got was signed more than twenty years ago. Would you have anything that old that Mr. Lopez might have signed?"

"He's been here a while. But not twenty years." She rummaged through the folder. "Hey, look at this."

It was Eduardo Lopez's original employment application: dated fifteen years ago, and typed on a manual. At the bottom was a signature.

"It's the same man."

"Son of a . . ." Marga whistled. "He always said he and his wife couldn't have children. You're telling me he has a daughter?"

"*Had* a daughter. He tell you that, that he couldn't have kids?"

"No, but I picked it up from what he— Wait. Yes. Yes, he did. I was over there, going through his bills. He was going on about why me and Ralph, the jerk, never had kids, 'cause he's real Catholic, and I turned it around on him. He said his wife couldn't have children."

"Marga," I said, "could I talk to him?"

When the door opened again, it was the man I'd seen shaping the cigars so expertly. He wore a ribbed tank undershirt and a pair of old corduroys with shiny wales. The huaraches on his feet were soled with tire-tread rubber. Despite the deep furrows in his skin and the crepe at his neck, Lopez's hair was still thick, and he kept it as neat and clean as he did his old clothes. Could I detect a bit of Felina's strong chin in his jawline, or was it just my imagination?

Marga stood behind him, putting one hand on his shoulder protectively. "Eduardo, this is Mr. O'Connor."

"Hello, Mr. Lopez."

No reaction. He peered at me, puzzled, his hands in front of him as if he were holding an invisible hat.

"I'm a friend of your daughter's."

Still no reaction. Lopez's face didn't change. I shot Marga a glance, but she shrugged. Did he speak English? Was this the right man?

"Mr. Lopez? You have a daughter named Felina?"

Nothing.

"Is Felina Lopez your daughter?"

Nothing.

"Mr. Lopez . . . Felina's dead."

He stared at me, and then the tears welled up in his eyes and his shoulders began to shake.

17

THE HUMIDITY HAD SKYROCKETED and the sun was a white-hot ball of hell hanging over Alameda Street. Eduardo Lopez followed me numbly down San Pedro. Once the tears and shaking had stopped, shock had set in and he had become scarily impassive. I was worried about Lopez and wanted to get him off filthy, urine-stinking San Pedro into someplace cool and quiet.

The only place I knew within walking distance was over on Sixth: a faux-proletarian hangout called Trotsky's, which supplied the remaining downtown loft dwellers with blini, omelettes, and Americanized Russian fare. Claudia liked it for Sunday brunch. Not the kind of place Eduardo Lopez would hang out, but I couldn't think of any other.

"Is this okay?"

He didn't say anything, but followed me inside like a bewildered puppy.

Trotsky's had a postmodern Marxist motif, designed to appeal to the sensibilities of the arugula-eating Bolsheviks who could afford a two-thousand-dollar-a-month loft. Old copies of *Pravda* were framed on the concrete walls, and the exposed ceiling ducts were hung with portraits of Lenin and banners marked in Cyrillic characters. Lopez plunked down in the nearest booth. I sat down opposite him gingerly.

"You all right, sir? You want some water?"

He shook his head no, and then shook it again, like a sleepwalker just coming to.

The waitress had a pierced tongue and crayon-yellow hair, but that didn't even seem to register with Lopez. I ordered two St. Petersburg omelettes and two iced teas. When she'd left, he bit his lip and looked across the table, fixing me with his one good eye.

"How do you know my Felina?"

"We were writing a book together."

"Felina was writing a book? My Felina?"

"Yes."

He processed that for a minute and then said, "But she is dead."

"Yes."

"I knew it." His voice was like dry leaves.

"I'm sorry."

Lopez stammered a few words in Spanish and rubbed the lip of the table with his thumb. "When?"

I was taken aback. Was it really possible Lopez hadn't heard or been told? Maybe. But then, Marga had told me he couldn't read, and he certainly wouldn't watch *Headline Journal* or *Hollywood Today!*

"About a month ago," I said. "She was living in Mexico. I'm sorry to break the news to you. I thought you must have known."

"No. No. Thank you. *Gracias* . . . Mexico . . . Were you with her?"

"No."

"Was there a priest?"

"I don't think so."

"She died alone?"

"I'm sorry."

"No one should have to . . . Oh, Felina," he whispered. "You were a good girl. You were such a good girl."

"I'm sorry. I didn't know her very well, but I'm sure she was a good woman."

Lopez shook his head. "She was a good *girl*. She got good marks. She made me dinner when I came home from work. Her mother was dead. We were all we had, each other. *Mi mija. Mija y Popi.*"

"I'm so sorry, Mr. Lopez."

"*Mija, mija.* Felina. She was so good then. Later she was . . ." A sigh. "Thank you for coming to tell me."

"You're welcome."

He combed his hair with his fingers, looking away. "How did you find me? She told you about me?"

"A little. She mentioned that her father was a cigar roller."

"We did not agree. I had not seen her for . . . Felina Maria. After her mother. She looked so much like her mother. I loved her so much . . . *Mija, mija.*"

He mumbled a few more words in Spanish. I waited. His voice finally dribbled away. He took a sip of iced tea.

"When was the last time you saw her, Mr. Lopez?"

The question seemed innocuous to me, but it shattered

Lopez. His mouth opened, and he began to weep, great silent sobs that wracked his body.

Our omelettes arrived at that moment, each topped with a blob of sour cream and tiny sturgeon roe that dotted the sour cream like tattoo ink. The waitress set the plates down timidly. "Is he, um . . ."

"He's fine. He just got some bad news. Thanks." I shot the nearby diners a look. They went back to posing. Lopez sobbed. I sat quietly and let it come.

When he was done, Lopez mumbled a silent prayer and made the sign of the cross. *"Lo siento,"* he said. "I am sorry."

"I understand. You loved her very much."

He shook his head no.

"Of course you did. Felina knew that."

More head shaking, violent this time. "She disgraced her mother's name. Felina Maria. I prayed for her to change. She lived with a man who sold drugs. She tried to give me money. I made her take it back. She was a whore, *ramera*—"

"Whatever Felina did, she's in heaven now. Right?"

He didn't reply.

"Mr. Lopez, please listen. Felina had stopped that. She was living in Mexico, writing a book. Whatever Felina might have done in her past, it's not your fault. You did the best you could."

Agony twisted his features, an agony I began to realize had less to do with Felina's death than their relationship while she was alive. "She told me she was not going to live. *Dios Mío* . . ."

Lopez was like a radio station, fading in and out of English. I was so busy trying to pick words out of his muttering that it took me a minute to process what he had just said. "Mr. Lopez—she *told* you she was—?"

He cut me off with another burst of Spanish. *Puta* and *que vergüenza*, he kept repeating—whore, shame. Then there was *Dios Mío*, and a word I couldn't understand; something that sounded like "seeda." Over and over again, those four phrases.

"Mr. Lopez—Mr. Lopez, please listen to me. She *knew* that it would happen? She told you she was going to die?"

"*Sí.*"

I touched the hem of his sleeve. "Felina *knew* that someone wanted to murder her?"

He stared at me, uncomprehending.

"I'm confused, sir. Felina died just a few weeks ago. When did you talk to her last?"

A long moment. He wiped his face with the flat of his hand, looking just as puzzled as I.

"I haven't spoken to Felina in five years."

The interior of the Buick was like a broiler oven. Nevertheless, I sat there in the U-Park, windows up, for nearly twenty minutes, trying to process the information that I had prized out of Eduardo Lopez.

A good reporter bird-dogs the parts of the story that don't make sense. Pieces stick out, just like one of Lopez's half-formed cigars. And it's those sticking-out pieces that demand your attention. They've either got to be nudged into place or chopped off.

The story of Felina Lopez and Dick Mann had pieces sticking out all over it, and I'd been in such a damn hurry to get the book done, to write the story that Jack Danziger wanted me to write, that I hadn't paid attention.

And the answer had been there all along, from the day I first met Felina Lopez in Tijuana; if I'd just taken the time, not to look at it, but really to *see* it, the same way I'd finally seen Jeff and Karen at the opening of Canem . . . the same way I'd finally seen Claudia and me.

The car was hot. I was breaking a sweat.

Felina had been murdered. It wasn't just a robbery gone wrong, though that might have been part of it. I knew who'd done it. And I knew who had wanted to get hold of my manuscript, and why.

What I didn't know was what I was going to do next.

I sat there sweating for ten more minutes, and then I started the car and drove over to Second and Spring.

The fourth floor was unusually quiet for a weekday. A few people were at their desks, but the usual white noise of a thousand fingers tapping a thousand keys was strangely muted. I weaved my way through the bullpens, saying hi to a few folks, noticing more pods vacant and empty. Reporters used to call the paper "The Velvet Coffin"—because so many talented writers landed there and ended up in cushy, benefit-laden oblivion. Now it just felt like a funeral home.

Fortunately, Sally was at the desk that she'd occupied for almost three decades, and her pod was a reassuring mess of printouts, reference books, old dummies, and a battered Coyote terminal with Post-Its stuck to its edges. She had an open container of Yoplait and a bottled water sitting on a stack of newspapers. Editor's lunch.

"Hey."

"Kieran!" She stopped typing and swiveled around. "Oh, God, I forgot to call you back. I'd take you to lunch, but I'm whomped again."

"Where is everybody? The garage was nearly empty, and this dump looks like a ghost town."

"At least ghost towns get a few tourists. This is pretty much it right now."

"Why is Barbara Kuhn's pod empty?"

"Barbara took the buyout. I thought you knew. Friday was her last day."

"Barbara had been here almost as long as you, Sal."

"Well, she's in Puerto Rico now for a month. She's thinking of trying to get a job on a small-town paper in Idaho or Utah. Now I'm doing her job as well as mine." Her voice dropped. "I might end up there myself. They wanted me to take the buyout, too, but I dug in my feet. Now I'm wondering if it was a mistake. They really want me out. But screw 'em. I'm tired of thinking about it. I'm sure you didn't come down to listen to me bitch." She smiled, but her eyes were tired. "So what was so important on the phone yesterday?"

"Nothing, really. I just came down to do a little research."

She waved her arm at the nearly empty bullpen. "Use Barbara's desk. Or pick a pod, any pod. It doesn't really matter much anymore."

"Okay. Thanks. Hey, is Roy Cruz still down on cityside?"

"Roy's still here. Some of us dinosaurs are hard to kill."

"Thanks, Sal."

———

Barbara's pod still had a working phone. I scared up some paper and pens and got down to it. First was a call to the library. I had them pull some clips from about five years ago. Library staff had been cut, too. The guy at the other end of the phone was busy, but promised to pull them right away.

I went up to the library. By the time the elevator had taken me down to cityside, I'd found what I suspected. But I still wanted to talk to Roy Cruz.

Roy had been at the paper even longer than Sally. His beat was LAPD headquarters. I was in luck: He was sitting at his desk in shirtsleeves and tie, reading his own stack of printouts.

"Roy? You have a minute?"

He squinted up at me. "Oh, Kieran. Sure. I just got back from Parker Center. What's up?"

Back in Barbara's pod, I took some deep breaths. Roy Cruz had confirmed what I suspected, and I knew what I had to do next.

I called 411 and got a number for an office in Century City.

"You have reached the offices of Levin Investigations. Please listen to the following options and, using your Touch-Tone pad, select the one—"

Screw it. I pressed 0.

"Levin Investigations," said a real live voice.

"Put Brooks on, would you?"

A huffy pause. "Who's calling for Mr. Levin, please?"

"Kieran O'Connor."

"Mr. Levin's not available, but if—"

"Look. He's been sending me messages for a while. If he's not there, call him. Or page him. Send up the Batsignal. I don't give a shit what you do. Just get hold of him and tell him I'll be at this number for exactly fifteen minutes."

Silence. After a moment, she asked, "What was that name again?"

I gave her Barbara's extension and sat back to wait.

Seven minutes later, the phone rang.

= 18 =

WHEN I WALKED BACK out to Spring Street, it was ninety-nine degrees and so smoggy I couldn't see the hills. The 10 was a sludgy river of metal heading west. By the time I passed Fairfax, though, traffic began to thin, and when I got off in downtown Santa Monica, it was seventy-five degrees, with a cool Pacific breeze. On the right day, you can sometimes remember why you bother to live in Southern California.

I found a quasi-legal spot on Broadway and jogged across the street to Palisades Park, a tiny strip of green that ran along the bluffs overlooking the Pacific Coast Highway.

Down below, joggers, Rollerbladers, and bicyclists shared the concrete path that curved through the sand. The Ferris wheel on the pier stood tall and still, a spare tire propped against the horizon. A lone box kite nipped at the sky. The sun hanging over the water was orange and sports-car red. From here, I could see all of Santa Monica Bay, from Rancho Palos Verdes up to the point at Malibu. A necklace of cars stretched up the Pacific Coast Highway, taillights heading home.

I put my hands on the railing and took a deep breath. My watch said 5:54.

I had six minutes, just enough time to make my appointment.

It was 5:59 by the time I reached the gazebo at Ocean and Idaho. But the person I'd come to meet was nowhere around. All I saw was a homeless guy asleep in the grass, a teenage couple tangled up under a picnic blanket, and a woman with a scarf who stared out to sea behind dark glasses. Down the walk, a Dumpster-diver was rummaging through a trash bin, stacking bright-green cans of Mountain Dew in his shopping cart.

New temporary fencing had been erected along the bluffs' edge here. The hillside was crumbling, slowly decaying from the annual rainstorms and the million little temblors that ran under our feet each day, invisible and unfelt. One day, miles under the earth, the wrong plate would shift a few inches, and the whole hillside would tumble across the highway and return to the sea.

"Hello, Kieran."

Materialized was the only word for it. One second he wasn't there, and the next he was standing in front of me, blocking out the fading sun.

Though I'd never even seen a picture of Brooks Levin, I knew him immediately. He was a good six-three, with beefy shoulders and large hands. He wore a nondescript blue blazer and a white shirt. Despite his cornerback build, there was something lithe and quick about him. Wire-rimmed glasses made his eyes look mild, even reproving. I had no idea where he'd come from. I could see why the guy had a nearly supernatural reputation.

"Where's your client?"

"Couldn't make it after all. So I'm standing in." The voice was the one I'd heard on the phone at the Wind & Sea, and it matched the body: understated but strong, and self-assured in the absolute.

I tried to control the rising panic I felt. "Is that supposed to scare me?"

"We need to talk."

"I came to talk to your client."

"You can tell me whatever you have to say."

"All right." I took two steps back from the edge of the bluff, away from Levin. "You said we need to talk? So talk."

"Why do you want to ruin his life?"

"Here's a better question, Levin. Why did you break into my room at the Beverly Hillshire?"

"I didn't break into your room, Kieran."

"So you paid someone else to do it. Sloan Baker probably let you in. I don't care how it happened. The end result was the same. You stole my manuscript."

He shrugged and didn't say anything.

"I'm outta here," I told him. "I didn't come to talk to you."

"Please hear me out." His voice was calm, eminently reasonable. "Think about what you're doing. How is making this public going to help anything? Felina is dead. It was just a matter of time. You're talking about ruining someone's life."

"That's not my problem. My job is to make sure the truth gets told."

A smile twitched the corners of his lips. "Spoken like a real reporter."

"I guess so. And that's *your* problem. See ya, Levin."

When I was several paces away, he called, "Hey."

I turned around.

Levin had his hand in his jacket. The hand came out with an envelope.

He held it out to me. The wind shifted and got colder. When I didn't move, he walked toward me, hand extended. The sun went behind a cloud, and salt spray hit my nose like ammonia.

"Take it," he said, amused. "Open it."

Inside was a bank draft, much like the one Shelly Nguyen had given me. Only this one had my name spelled correctly, and this one was for a lot more money. More money, in fact, than I'd gotten for the book. And, as the anti-conscience in the back of my head whispered, fifteen percent of this one didn't have to go to Jocelyn.

"It's a gift. For publishing your book. Just as written. It's fine the way it is. You'll sell a lot of copies, and no more lives have to be ruined." He put his hand on my shoulder. "Be reasonable. Let it go."

"Levin, let me repeat: I didn't come here to talk to you."

He sighed and looked out to sea, not removing his hand from my shoulder.

"All right," he said after a moment.

Disappointed, shaking his head, Levin walked back down the path and stopped at the gazebo. He leaned down and spoke to the woman in the dark glasses. She got up, brushing her hands against her slacks, and walked over to me. Levin disappeared behind the gazebo. When she got close, I could see that the hair under the scarf was a wig.

"Hello, Betty," I said.

"You're going to ruin my son's life?" she said.

"This isn't tabloid gossip. I have to tell what I know."

"Richie already lost his father. You want him to lose his mother, too? Jesus Christ Almighty. You people are sick. Beyond sick." Betty took off her glasses. Her eyes were puffy and red.

"It's not my fault. It's yours. You made him lose both of his mothers."

She opened her mouth, but all that came out was a sharp, knifelike gasp of air.

"People knew Richie was adopted, Betty. Sloan Baker told me the first time I met her. And the adoption wasn't quiet. The two of you even did a spread in *Celeb,* welcoming home the new baby. You might have been able to keep his picture out of the press for a while, but he's in school now. It can't go on forever. The older he gets, the more he'll look like his father. What were you planning to do then?"

She covered her mouth, trying to stop her hyperventilation. Betty Bradford Mann wasn't acting now. She simply wasn't that good an actor.

"And the damnedest part is: Felina didn't tell me she was Richie's mother. You must have read that manuscript by now. If anything, she *protected* you and your family."

"You don't *understand*."

"Then explain it."

"She wanted him back. She wanted him *back*." Betty took a deep breath, pressing her hand against her chest.

"Custody?"

Betty nodded.

"How did you get custody in the first place?"

"This all started about six years ago. Dick and I were having problems. He was seeing Felina. It didn't last long. We patched it up. Then she called him and said she was two months pregnant. I didn't know what to do. Dick was upset, but he couldn't stand the thought of . . ."

"So you agreed to buy the baby."

"Not buy. Adopt. We got her out of L.A. After Richie was born, we gave her enough money to get out of our lives forever. She used it to buy that house. I thought we'd never hear from her again. That was part of the deal. Then Dick died. And she called me.

"I thought she wanted more money, but she didn't. She said that now that Dick was gone, she wanted Richie back. She said he needed to be with his real mother." Betty glared at me. "I *am* that child's real mother."

"My God. You would have won in any court. With your money and her past? You didn't have to kill her."

"I didn't mean to! I didn't take her seriously. All she had was that house. She didn't have enough money to hire any lawyers. I told her that. I told her to leave me alone. And then she called back the next week and told me she was going to write a book for Danziger Press, for a lot of money."

Betty reached into her pocket for a cigarette, but the pack

was empty. Her hands were shaking. She dropped it. A puff of wind carried it over the bluff.

"That woman was going to use her book advance to fight me in court. I begged her to think of Richie. I told her that everything in her past would come out in court. He lost his father; now he needs to see the two of us mud-wrestling in front of some judge? I thought I got through to her. But then she called me again. She'd signed the contract and the book was on. So I went down to Mexico to talk to her, to try and shake some sense into her. But I swear to God, I never meant to kill her. It just happened."

"What 'just happened'?"

"I'd taken as much money as I could with me. She'd been bribed once, I figured she could be bribed again. But she was firm. She wanted Richie back. I asked her, How can you have him *back* when you never had him in the first place? It started as an argument. Then it turned into a fight. A real fight. We were rolling around on the floor. I don't know what happened. I swear to God, I still don't know what happened. It was only seconds. But she was dead. It happened. It just happened. And then I got out of there as soon as I could."

"When you adopted Richie, you really thought you'd never have to deal with Felina again? It never occurred to you she might come back for him?"

She sighed, weighing how much to tell me. It didn't matter; I knew it all now anyway.

"Felina had just found out she was very sick. We thought it was— We thought she didn't have very long."

"But she got better instead."

"Yes. She got better. She thought she was cured."

"What was wrong with her?"

"Cancer. Breast cancer. Frankly, we didn't think she had more than a year or two to live."

"Don't bullshit me anymore, Betty. Felina didn't have breast cancer."

Eduardo Lopez had told me. The word he kept repeating—the word I heard as "seeda"—wasn't a word at all. Roy Cruz had translated it. It was an acronym. *SIDA. Síndrome de inmuno deficiencia adquirida.*

Felina must have gone to Mexico desperate for a cure. I'd seen the pills, the vitamins, the Zuni fetishes. Walking through the streets, I'd also seen the black-market *farmacias* that dispensed all kinds of herbs and snake oil, along with dubious versions of protease inhibitors and AZT. Tailor-made for a desperate woman with a New Age bent.

But there are some things in life that a handful of herbs and *la águila* can't cure.

The sun went behind another cloud, turning the bay from blue-green to gunmetal gray. False dusk.

"Did Dick have it?" I asked.

No response.

"Do you?"

"No." Performance or not? I couldn't tell anymore.

"Does Richie?"

Betty started to cry again. "Why are you doing this to us? I'm not a homicidal maniac. I'm not. Until that night, I'd never thought I was capable of—"

"Is that little boy HIV-positive?"

Her head jerked up in a fury.

"*Why?* If I told you he was, would it make one damn bit of difference? Would it change what you intend to do to us?"

Would it?

If I told the police what I knew, a woman would go to jail and leave her child parentless. That was tough, but that was Betty Mann's own fault. I could live with that.

But if that child was terminally ill, could I take him away from the one person in his life who could offer him love and stability and the financial means for a healthy life?

And if I did, just for the sake of a story that never was important in the first place, was I any better than Betty Mann herself? Or Felina Lopez? Or Leo Lazarnick?

Once everything I knew about reporting seemed forged in steel, stark as black and white. A binary system: truth and lies. One was good; the other, bad. But now the world and my place in it were shades of gray that kept shifting. *The rules have changed,* Gina Guglielmelli had told me, laughing. And they had. At least the tab reporters of the world had their own bedrock beliefs, sleazy as they were. Once I thought I had a value system, too, but my beliefs were no more solid than the bluffs where I stood.

"Would it make a difference?" Betty demanded. "Would it?"

"I don't know."

Eduardo Lopez was a good man who had loved Felina. He was also a terrible father who had rejected his daughter at the time she needed him most. Betty Mann was a woman who had committed the worst crime imaginable. She was also, without a doubt, a good mother. And her fate, and the fate of a little boy, lay in my hands, and I felt like a toddler holding a hand grenade.

"I think so," I said slowly. "Yes, I think it would make a difference."

"It would?"

"Not for you. For him. They're your sins. Not his."

Something in the air between us shifted.

"I believe you," she said. "God help me, I shouldn't, but I believe you."

A couple walked past hand in hand. We were silent for a moment.

"So. Is he?" I asked gently.

Betty closed her eyes. A jogger went past, sneakers slapping against the wet grass. She waited until he was out of earshot. The taut balloon of tension between us had dissipated. All the air was gone.

"He's been tested every six months since he was born. And he's fine. We both are."

"I'm glad."

"Thank you."

Her voice was a whisper. False dusk was gone. The light was fading for real now, and the lifeguard shacks on the beach stretched long shadows across the sand.

I handed back the envelope.

"I guess that's what I needed to know," I told her, and walked away down the darkening bluffs.

= 19 =

SILLY SEASON, WE CALLED IT: the long, hot California summer and the outrageous media circuses that it spawned like hurricanes. Vernon Ash's trial was a silly season story. So were the deaths of Felina Lopez and Dick Mann. But when Betty Bradford Mann surrendered to authorities at the end of that summer, silly season reached a pitch of unprecedented proportions.

First, there were the legal questions to be straightened out. An American citizen had allegedly murdered (even in my own mind, I was saying *allegedly*) another American citizen on Mexican soil. That was already a few years' work for a minor galaxy of bilingual lawyers. Susan D'Andrea and her ilk hit the ground spin-doctoring. And the tabloids, which had already put Dick Mann and Felina Lopez's deaths on the back burner, sank their chops into Act III of the drama, which promised to be the juiciest yet.

In the synod of *Headline Journal* watchers and *Celeb* readers, I knew there would be no doubt as to who was the wronged party here. Betty Bradford Mann wasn't a television actress to them; she was a maltreated widow trying to raise her son the best she could. Felina Lopez was a greedy hooker who wasn't just satisfied with Betty's husband; she had to have her son, too. If Felina ended up with a toe tag instead of custody—well, it wasn't right, but it wasn't completely unjustified, either.

"Lana Turner," Lydia told me. "With Douglas Sirk directing. Lots of great suffering scenes, lots of great costumes. Ann Blyth or Dorothy Malone in the Felina part." She sighed. "But they don't make movies like that anymore. And *that's* why I watch Court TV, Kieran."

Lydia had a point. I wasn't surprised, a few days later, when I picked up a copy of *Biz* and saw that a cable network had commissioned a script for *Desperate Measures: The Betty Bradford Mann Story*.

An arraignment date was set. The legal teams fought for position. And a nation of Madame Defarges sat back, taking up remote controls instead of knitting needles, and waited.

This was the Zeitgeist—at least, what I was able to glean when I looked up from my computer. I had a book to revise and rewrite.

At the end of the week, I'd written 125 more pages. This time it flowed. Maybe it wasn't a story worth telling, but I felt I'd told it well.

And Jack Danziger threw a dinner party to celebrate.

The guest list was petite, at my insistence: just Jack, Kitty, Elise, her partner Beth, Jocelyn, and me. Jack had wanted to invite "just *one* columnist," but I'd put my Converse high-topped foot down. I didn't want to dress up and I damn sure didn't want to answer any questions. Jocelyn had already suggested that I take on a publicist "just for a couple of months, Peaches," but I put my foot down there, too, so she stayed busy earning her fifteen percent by fending off all media requests for interviews.

Claudia begged off the night of the party. She was too busy with Café Canem, or so she claimed, and I didn't press the issue. That night, I pulled on a T-shirt and shorts and drove out to Hancock Park, Lydia chattering away in the passenger seat.

As it turned out, I couldn't have made a better choice of dinner partner. Kitty and Jack were captivated by her, and she by them. I shoveled Elise's eggplant lasagna into my face and said barely a word through the whole dinner.

"What I still don't get," I said when the sorbet arrived, "was how Frank Grassley got my name."

"What do you mean?" asked Jocelyn.

"We'd kept the book under wraps to that point. Felina's murder hadn't even made the paper. Hell, Jack was thinking about invoking *force majeure* and canceling the whole project. Then Grassley called Jack, out of the blue. He knew about the project and he knew I was working on it. Up till then, it had been a secret, remember? And the next day, *Headline Journal* showed up at my front door and all hell broke loose."

"He's a reporter, Kieran," said Lydia. "Y'all have your sources."

"Yeah, but Grassley's not a *good* reporter. I mean, he must have gotten a tip, but . . . it's just puzzling."

"It doesn't matter, dear, does it?" said Kitty. "After all, it saved the project."

I narrowed my eyes at her. A conversation floated back to

me, a conversation we'd had in the parking garage at Danziger Press: *Let me see what I can do, then . . . The book will happen. One way or another. I promise.*

"Kitty . . ."

She looked up and smiled her batty old-lady smile at Elise. "Dear, this sorbet is just wonderful. You're going to have to get me the recipe."

Two days later, Lydia went back to Louisiana. The official explanation was that the house had gone to hell in her absence, but I knew better. All she'd wanted was a little attention, and once she'd gotten it, she found that she genuinely missed Charlie, Teddy, and Melinda. She had a business to run and a family to tyrannize. Her departure made the apartment seem empty.

Empty, of course, for Claudia and me.

Even then we never discussed what had happened.

Sometimes you don't realize that you've been adrift for years, until one day when you look up and find you can't see land anymore. Claudia had just realized the truth before I did. It was no one's fault, really. I was still naive when it came to relationships, and a little 'commitment-challenged,' but I knew that we'd always love each other, even if we weren't in love with each other. Perhaps that had been our strongest bond all along.

A few book offers came Jocelyn's way, but I didn't want to think about them for a while. Instead, I spent my last free days before the publication of *Mann's Woman* walking on the beach, taking in a few movies, and playing with my new computer. I still went to the corner and got the paper every morning, but these days I found myself throwing out everything but the real-estate listings.

There was a one-bedroom over in Ocean Park that sounded good, and a loft space down in the canyon that would be available in a month or two. Brenner had even offered to put me up in his spare room for a while, but I wasn't really in any hurry.

Claudia's couch was more comfortable than the one at the Beverly Hillshire anyway.

I was lying on Claudia's couch one morning wearing her old Saints jersey and playing on the laptop, when the doorbell rang.

The woman on the porch was twenty-six or twenty-seven, with floppy brown hair that hung down into her eyes. She wore a dark suede blazer over a man's dress shirt and a pair of boots. Her build was average, with the exception of a chunky butt that filled out her jeans. Under her arm was a large cast-iron stew pot.

We looked at each other for a long, appraising moment, and I felt something in the base of my spine begin to stir and tickle.

"For you," she said, and handed me the stew pot.

I lifted the lid. Steam curled. Squiggles of fusilli floated on top of the broth, and a divine aroma of vegetables and herbs drifted up with the steam.

"Minestrone," the woman said. "I made it myself last night."

"Smells great."

We hadn't taken our eyes off each other.

Finally, she laughed and took a tape recorder out of her bag. "Well, do I have to stand out here all day, O'Connor?"

I laughed, too, and then I stepped back and invited Gina Guglielmelli in.